ISTVÁN ÖRKÉNY (1912–1979) is one of the most popular and most often read writers of post-war Hungary. His first volume of short stories, *Ocean Dance,* appeared in 1941. During the war while serving on the Russian Front, Örkény was taken prisoner and sent to a camp near Moscow. Here he wrote the play *Voronezh,* the sociographic *People of the Camps* and a series of biographical pieces, *Those Who Remember.* The latter was smuggled into Hungary by a camp inmate and published shortly before Örkény's return home in 1946. This established him as one of Hungary's leading writers. After the war, Örkény's writing appeared in quick succession, short stories, novellas, novels and plays. Örkény's continuing popularity with readers was established by his *One Minute Stories* which he continued writing till the end of his life. The present edition is the first comprehensive collection of *One Minute Stories* to be published in English.

JUDITH SOLLOSY has a degree in English literature from Columbia University. Since 1975 she has been living in Budapest, where she is senior editor at Corvina Books. Her drama and short story translations have appeared in books and periodicals in the US, the UK, Canada and Australia. Her latest translations include Péter Esterházy's *The Book of Hrabal* (1993), *A Little Hungarian Pornography* (1995) by the same author, and Endre Ady's *Neighbours of the Night* (1994).

Dear Rik,

This is a collection of short stories that show very well the Hungarian spirit and humor.
For You, if you want to remember.

I believe I am very lucky to know You and be able to learn from You a lot of things, like being brave, honest and 100% fair.
I will miss You very much.

Thanks for these 4 years, and I wish You and your family all the best in your new „life".

Tsanett Szendy

Budapest, July 9.

ISTVÁN ÖRKÉNY

one minute
stories

selected and translated by

judith sollosy

CORVINA

This collection of *One Minute Stories*
has been compiled from the following volumes of István Örkény:
Egyperces novellák, Magvető Kiadó, Budapest, 1977
Egyperces novellák, Szépirodalmi Könyvkiadó, Budapest, 1984
Visszanézve, Szépirodalmi Könyvkiadó, Budapest, 1985
Búcsú. Kiadatlan novellák, Szépirodalmi Könyvkiadó, Budapest, 1989

Fifth printing 1999

This edition first published in Hungary by Corvina Books Ltd.,
Budapest, Vörösmarty tér 1
in co-operation with Brandl & Schlesinger of Sydney

Cover design by Gábor Váradi
Cover art by Garry Shead

ISBN 963 13 4783 4

Printed and bound in Hungary
by Stádium Printing House

contents

introduction

It is hardly surprising that Hungarians have the reputation of being great survivors. They have been obliged to learn the arts of survival throughout the turbulent history of that little landlocked European country which has experienced more than its fair share of invasion, revolution and repression. István Örkény, the author of these wry sketches, saw in his lifetime a bewildering succession of political systems replacing each other, each demanding absolute and unwavering loyalty.

Örkény was born in 1912, during the last days of the Austro-Hungarian Empire. By the time of his death in 1979 he would have experienced a brief but bloody Bolshevik uprising, a right-wing totalitarian regime under the Regent Admiral Horty (the regent of a country without a monarch or a navy) which was followed, with only a brief interlude, by a succession of brutal strongmen answering to Moscow's bidding. He lived through the futile uprising of 1956 and also, in the years just before his death in 1979, the emergence of a more benign "goulash socialism" that paved the way for the bloodless revolution of 1989 which brought Communism to an end. Like millions of his compatriots, or at least those who did not manage at one time or another to slip past heavily guarded borders, he would have heard each of these regimes insisting, with the stridency of

Central or Eastern European political rhetoric, that it and it alone was capable of insuring peace, prosperity and the pursuit of happiness. He would have seen ancient hatreds and enmities persisting despite the repeated declarations of a brave new world, and he would have realized (again, along with his fellow Hungarians) that the powerful, the determined and the brutal had an uncanny ability to preserve their privileges. The remainder of the population had to survive as best they could: by evolving a tongue-in-cheek cynical scepticism and an ability to find a way around "Keep Out!" signs, by learning constant vigilance, trusting few and confiding in none, and above all, by constantly reminding themselves that all political creeds, indeed, creeds of all kinds, are essentially absurd.

People of Örkény's generation became past-masters at such arts, especially if they lived in Budapest, that raffish, cynical metropolis, a "western" city on the edge of Eastern Europe. In the twenties and thirties, and indeed up to the dark days of 1943 and 1944 (and probably also in later years) a particular Budapest "style" emerged, brittle, irreverent, perhaps even a trifle irresponsible. In a mad world, it provided the only sane response, that of laughter.

Örkény's little stories, which proved immensely popular in Hungary, managed to laugh at the absurdities (and also the horrors) of that world in such a genial and oblique way that he remained more-or-less untouched even during periods of the most repressive censorship, when many of Hungary's best writers were silenced, imprisoned or forced to go underground. His books continued to be published and his plays performed largely, I suspect, because of their feline sophistication. Irony, allusiveness and obliquity have always been the best ways of pulling the wool over the eyes of literal-minded officialdom, both of the left and of the right.

In one sense these stories and sketches are intensely Hungarian, or better still, pervaded by the particular flavor of life in Budapest. Here is a world of gossip and innuendo, a world of cafés and intrigue, a city where long-established social rituals and prejudices survived changes of regime, a world where petty bureaucrats have always strutted in the confidence of their power, yet had, each of them, their particular price. A depressing world, certainly, but also one with a curious exhilaration. Örkény's sketches and anecdotes, here published for the first time in English, provide a wonderful introduction to a city and its inhabitants, who have always managed to spring back, cheeky, irreverent, wholly without illusions, no matter how brutally repressed or violently pushed down. Though they contain nothing of the heroic or the grandiose, these stories are nevertheless a testimony to resilience, to an ability to laugh even at those times when it would be easier to cry.

They also reveal the sophistication of much Hungarian writing of recent decades. Perhaps because Hungarians speak a language practically without affinities with any of the major European languages, Hungarians have always been obliged to be more outward-looking than those of us fortunate (or unlucky) enough to live in one of the great linguistic communities of the world. In these little tales, despite their intense "Hungarianness", the astute will catch echoes of that cosmopolitanism that has marked the best of Hungarian culture in the twentieth century, echoes of Borges and Calvino and perhaps even of The New Yorker at its best. Örkény's great gift, a gift shared by several of his compatriots, was to endow a richly urband and universal culture with a distinctly Hungarian accent. And, as always, there is a wry elusiveness, a cunning capacity to say shocking things with disarming innocence, which is one of the hallmarks of a master of the arts of survival.

Andrew Riemer
Sydney, January 1994

handling instructions

Despite their brevity, the stories in this book have a certain amount of literary merit. They also have the added advantage of saving us time. While the soft-boiled egg is boiling or the number you are dialing answers (provided it is not engaged, of course) you have ample time to read one of these short stories which, because of their brevity, I have come to think of as one minute stories. You can read them whatever your mood, whether you are sitting down or standing up, in fine weather or in foul. They even make good reading on a crowded bus. Most can be enjoyed on a walk.

Do pay attention to the titles, though! The author strove for brevity, which put a special burden of responsibility on him when choosing the titles for his stories, of which they form an organic part.

But do not stop at the titles! First the title, then the story. It's is the only proper manner of handling.

Attention! If something is not clear to you, reread the story is question. If it is still not clear to you, dump the story, the fault lies with the author. There are no dim-witted readers, only badly written one minute stories.

the grotesque
(a practical approach)

Stand with your legs apart. Bend forward. Look back between your legs. Thank you.

Now look around you and take stock of what you see. The world has been stood on its head. The gentlemen's feet beat about in the air while the ladies, she how they grab for their skirts? The cars, too: their four tires are spinning in the air, looking for all the world like a dog trying to scratch its stomach. Then there's the chrysanthemum, its thin jack-in-the-box stem reaching for the sky as it balances precariously on its head – and the express train speeding along on top of its trail of smoke.

To the left, the parish church stands balanced on the tips of the lightning rods sticking out of its twin steeples. And over there is a sign on the window of a pub:

FRESH BEER ON TAP!

Inside, a customer, his head to the floor, staggers laboriously from the counter, holding a mug of beer in his hand. Do notice the order, though: the foam is at the bottom, the beer is on the top, and the bottom of the mug is on top of the beer. Yet not a drop is spilled.

Is it winter? You bet your life! Just look at the snowflakes as they flutter up, and the skaters as they zigzag in pairs, dangling from the icy mirror of the sky. Not an easy sport, skating!

However, let us look for a merrier spectacle. Ah, there! A funeral! Amidst the snowflakes falling up, through the veil of tears trickling the other way around, we can see the gravediggers haul the coffin up with two hefty ropes. The colleagues, friends and relations of the deceased, both near and far, his widow and three orphans, all grab some clods of earth and begin pelting the coffin. Let us recall the heartrending sound as the clods of earth are flung into a grave, knock against the coffin and break into tiny little pieces. The grieving widow sobs. The poor fatherless orphans wail.

How different it feels to throw things up! How much more dexterity it takes to hit the coffin! To start with, you need high quality clods, otherwise they disintegrate halfway up. So there is much grabbing, shoving and running helter-skelter to retrieve the most compact pieces. But a good clod of earth is not enough. Badly aimed, it falls back down and if it should hit somebody, especially a rich, distinguished relative, there is no escaping the titter of delight that follows. However, if all goes well and the clod of earth is firm and compact, the aim is accurate and on the mark, the man who flung it is applauded, and everyone goes home feeling happy. For days to come people talk about the perfect aim, the charming deceased, and the amusing ceremony, how splendid it turned out, and they do so with no trace of hypocrisy, feigned lamentation or pretense at sympathy.

And now, you may straighten up. As you see, the world is on its feet again, and you are at liberty to mourn your dearly departed with all the tears and dignity you can muster.

november

The morning fog was heavy, the traffic slow. The tram had pulled out right in front of Kordova Kordován's nose. The forty-year-old salad chef of the Restaurant Royale stood waiting at the stop. After a while he got fed up with standing around and so, with his right hand he took a firm grip of his left thumb and with a quick jerk, pulled it off. Taking it between two fingers he studied it, wrapped it up in a clean handkerchief, and reaching inside his coat, slipped it securely in the rear pocket of his trousers. He looked around. The next tram still hadn't come. But Kordova Kordován just shrugged. He wasn't about to get worked up over every little trifle.

c l a s s i f i e d
a d v e r t i s e m e n t
(nostalgia)

Must urgently exchange two-room, third floor apartment with built-in kitchen cabinets on Joliot Curie Square over-looking Eagle Peak for two-room, third floor apartment with built-in kitchen cabinet on Joliot Curie Square overlooking Eagle Peak. Money no object.

inquiry into the state of my health

"Hello!"

"Hello, there!"

"How are you?"

"Very well, thank you. And you?"

"Couldn't be better."

"Neither could I."

"What's that you're dragging behind you then? It looks just like a rope!"

"Oh, that! That's no rope! That's my guts!"

n o n f a t a l   a c c i d e n t

During the afternoon rush hour, on one of the busiest streets of Tokyo two hara-kiri were involved in a head-on collision. Luckily, the outcome of the accident was not fatal. Except for a few minor scrapes and scratches plus the fright they'd had, the hara-kiri suffered no major injuries.

stubborn misprint
(corrigendum)

Last Tuesday our paper reported that the Swedish Academy of Sciences has awarded an honorary doctorate to a Hungarian scientist whose name, much to our regret, we mistakenly printed in the headline as Dr. Peter Paul Paulpeter. Dr. Peter Paul Paulpeter's name appeared erroneously in our article as well. The name of the distinguished physicist should have read Dr. Peter Paul Paulpeter.

fifties news item

Miner Márton Haris, a resident of the mining town of Borsodbánya, got into bed last night, slipped between the sheets, lit a cigarette, smoked it down to the stub, switched off the light, turned to the wall, and fell fast asleep.

life should
be so simple

1. remove fire extinguisher from bracket
2. open valve
3. approach source of fire
4. extinguish fire
5. close valve
6. replace extinguisher on bracket

i n c i d e n t

A paraffin cork that was just like any other paraffin cork (he said his name was Alexander G. Hirr, Jr., but what's in a name?) fell into the water. For some time it just bopped up and down on the surface. But then a strange thing happened. Gradually, almost imperceptibly, it began to sink until it reached the bottom and was never heard from again. No explanation for the baffling incident has yet been offered.

a   h e a r t f e l t   c a l l

a heartfelt call, a grudging sigh
addressed to a piece of iron
of unspecified function
that weathered the storms
of history
lying low and quiet-like
in a crate chock full of junk
because neither our grandfathers
nor our fathers
had the guts to chuck it out
onto the junk pile
nor will those to come
after me*

*(You'll outlive me, you little twirp) (I.Ö.)

c l i m a x

The janitor was the first to notice the smell. He broke down the door. He spotted the farewell note on the stone floor of the kitchen. It was tucked under a small ceramic ashtray holding the butt of the victim's last cigarette. IT IS MY FIFTY-FIRST BIRTHDAY, it said. THE TENANTS DO NOT LIKE ME. THE LANDLORD REFUSES TO FIX MY LEAKY TAP. I WANT TO DIE. (Signed:) Mrs. Mihály Berger. The cigarette butt bore traces of fresh lipstick.

official statement
by the society
for the prevention
of cruelty to animals

Thanks to a long and heated debate championed by the members of our Society, the Rabbit Stew and Fish Soup Plant has just inaugurated a new workshop dedicated to opening the newly sealed tins.

At the new workshop which is called The Can Opener the newly canned tins of rabbit stew and fish soup are reopened, drained of liquid, and the chunks of meat and fish are reconstituted and taken back to their original habitat, where they are released.

We herewith wish to express our sincere gratitude to the management of the Rabbit Stew and Fish Soup Plant who have at last come to understand the true meaning of humanitarianism.

a h a s u e r u s*

Two Jews are walking down the street.
The first Jew asks the second a question.
The second Jew answers him.
The two Jews continue walking.
The first Jew who in the meantime has thought
        of another question asks it.
The second Jew answers him.
Sometimes this amuses them.
Sometimes it does not.
And so the two Jews continue walking.
They also continue talking.
Life, as you can see, is not always a bowl of cherries.

---

* Ahasuerus was the Old Testament king who, having given his deputy
Haman permission for the massacre of the Jews, was persuaded by
Queen Esther to save them.

v a r i a t i o n s

do not walk on the grass
on the grass on the grass
don't you try and trespass
oh, no, not on the grass
you can't
you mustn't
not there
don't!

in memoriam dr. h.g.k.

"Hölderlin ist ihnen unbekannt?"* Dr. H.G.K. asked as he dug the pit for the horse's carcass.

"Who is that?" the German guard growled.

"The author of *Hyperion*," said Dr. H.G.K., who had a positive passion for explanations. "The greatest figure of German Romanticism. How about Heine?" he tried again.

"Who're them guys?" the guard growled, louder than before.

"Poets," Dr. H.G.K. said. "But Schiller. Surely you have heard of Schiller?"

"That goes without saying," the German guard nodded.

"And Rilke?" Dr. H.G.K. insisted.

"Him, too," the German guard said and, turning the color of paprika, shot Dr. H.G.K. in the back of the head.

---

* You're not familiar with Hölderlin? *(Germ.)*

a b o u q u e t
o f b a n a l i t i e s

(for Zsuzsa)

why beat about the bush
you're the apple of my eye
when you're away
absence makes the heart grow fonder
though who would have thought
there's no way of telling, really
it's all due to blind chance, anyhow
it happened long ago in never-never land
when hand in hand
shoulder to shoulder
we braced ourselves
to face the vicissitudes of life

the tough part though is yet to come
'cause mother nature
she don't mess around
come winter the mountains are snow-clad
in spring the trees burst into bloom
and in autumn the leaves must fall
so don't count your chickens before they're hatched
the swift chariot of time flies whizzing past
and life is but a dream
so make hay while the sun shines
death from whence no traveller returns
will get the better of us you'll see

the cards are stacked to here
but once the door is shut behind us
life will go on its merry way
others will follow in our footsteps
as many as grains of sand in the desert
living their own lives

till death do us part
feet rooted firmly to the ground
with a sense of loss
will they remember us

imperfect conjugation

often I just stare at nothing
often you just stare at nothing
often he/she/it just stares at nothing
often we just stare at nothing, etc., etc., etc.

a number of variations
on the theme
of self-realization

Why deny it. As a child I entertained the usual foolish dreams. For instance, I wanted to be a pilot, an engine driver, or failing that, an engine. Sometimes I even fantasized that when I grew up I'd become the Orient Express.

A distant relative, the titular abbot Dr. Kniza, a highly educated and sober-minded gentleman, tried to talk me into becoming a pebble. To tell the truth, the finality, the rounded-out silence held a certain fascination for me. But Mom wanted just the opposite. She wanted me to find something related to time. "You go and be an egg, son," she'd urge me now and again. "An egg is birth and death all at once. It is time passing in a fragile shell. Anything can come of an egg," she reasoned.

But man proposes, God disposes and so here I am, sand in an hourglass, possibly so both Uncle Kniza and Mom should have their wish. After all, sand is timelessness incarnate and the hourglass is the ancient symbol of mortality. It even crops up in Egyptian hieroglyphics where it means "the sun's on it's way down, buddy!" "gosh, how time doth fly over the pyramids," "the migrating mynah birds are gathering without a permit again," and "what's that pain in the pit of my stomach, Doctor Nephros?"

It is not easy landing such a comfortable job. But

let it be said to Uncle Kniza's credit that even though he disapproved of me compromising my principles in this way, he pulled some strings and I was hired on a temporary basis. I am temporary because I am used only for cooking eggs, so Mom was right on two counts, I guess.

For some time everything went smoothly and I was beginning to think I'd managed to make a very pleasant life for myself. That's when calamity struck. From one day to the next I got lumpy, which for sand is as disastrous as a beer-gut is for a belly dancer. I manage to squeeze my legs through somehow but my backside keeps getting stuck in the bottleneck with alarming frequency. I've tried going down head first, but the fact is I still don't come out ahead, if you know what I mean. There I am squirming and writhing for all I'm worth for what seems like hours. The eggs stop cooking, the hourglass comes to a standstill, and all those grains of sand wait helpless above my head. They do not rush me in any way, mind you. Still, their patience is just like a mute reproach and it is driving me nuts. I can't even pretend it's not my fault because it is. I must have had a tendency to go lumpy all along. The truth is I'm just a reckless, rebellious, unsociable fellow patently unfit for sand.

At such times, all sorts of things come to mind. Anyone who sees me today would never believe it but I could have become a vacuum in a light-bulb! And there was a girl too a pretty though silly creature called Panni who was employed at the Batiste & Silk Works. Anyhow, one day she turned to me and said, "Listen, why don't you come with me and we'll make a pair of ladies' panties out of you?" I was deeply offended at the time. But in my present predicament, her offer seems like an answer to my prayers. Even if being a pair of ladies' underpants is not what you'd call a challenge, it's got a certain *je ne sais quoi* about it, if you know what I mean.

Instead I am stuck in the bottleneck again from which place I wish to inform all those who I may have disappointed that though I received nothing but bad advice from my loved ones, I have no one to blame but myself. I shouldn't have settled for this dull but secure existence. Had I been a little more adventurous, with a bit of luck I might have made something of myself. After all, if the engineer who designed the Queen Mary had thought of me instead, I wouldn't have to pull in my stomach now in order to squeeze through this damned isthmus but riding on top of fifty-foot waves, defying the elements, I'd be sailing the oceans with mast held proudfully high.

One fine day Victor T. was sent into outer space. He was not the first astronaut to be so honored but he was the first artist. He was away for six days. Halfway there they asked him what he'd prefer to see, the rings of the planet Saturn or the spots of the sun.

"It makes no difference," Victor T. answered. "Why don't you decide?"

In that case they are going to show him the spots of the sun, they said. A painter should find them of more interest.

"Possibly," Victor T. agreed.

After his return, Victor T. was greeted by a group of excited journalists waiting for him at the Cosmos Airport Restaurant. But he sat in their midst wrapped in dogged silence, his face the image of unutterable boredom. Instead of answering their questions, Victor T. stared hard at an orange one of the reporters was peeling.

But a few weeks later, his painterly style underwent a dramatic transformation. On his celebrated olive and billiard ball still-lifes (from his so-called "olive-green" period) there now appeared the first orange.

In his later years, Victor T. turned to lemons as well and later still, hens' eggs. But the orange was never absent from any of his works.

This is when Victor T. turned into a truly great artist.

a f f i d a v i t

I have reached the end of my tether. I keep dialing the wrong number. When I talk to my superiors my voice trembles. I have (so to speak) lost my initiative. My teenage daughter does not respect me. Come next year I will turn fifty.

In view of the above I, Dr. Rudolph Stü the undersigned, hereby solemnly declare that the signature on this document is a forgery and the signatory a fraud with whom I have nothing in common.

Dr. Rudolph Stü

optical illusion

Dr. Géza Dobrolubimov, the eminent professor of physics at Budapest University and recipient of numerous state awards, died early this morning of a cerebral haemorrhage. His students had jokingly referred to him as "Spotty" because summer and winter he had the eccentric habit of wearing white suits with red polka dots. It did not come to light until after the autopsy that the renowned man of science was not eccentric at all and did not deserve the ridicule of his students. His mother, who was inordinately fond of red polka dot bed linen, once mistook some dots for a baby, diapered them, fed them and brought them up as her own. During the ensuing sixty-nine years, all of Budapest fell prey to this amusing optical illusion.

Dr. Dobrolubimov's remains, approximately two dozen spots, will be laid to rest tomorrow at noon in a grave donated by a grateful city.

the careless driver

Supply man József Pereszlényi brought his Wartburg (license plate No. CO 75-14) to a halt in front of the corner newspaper stand.

"Give me today's *Budapest Herald*," he said.

"I'm all out."

"Give me yesterday's then."

"I'm all out of yesterday's too. But I happen to have tomorrow's."

"Has it got the movie guide?"

"They all do."

"Fine. Give me tomorrow's then." Having said that, Pereszlényi got back in his car. He found the movie guide. After a while he spotted a Czechoslovak film, *The Loves of a Blond*,* which he'd heard was worth seeing. It was playing at the Blue Lagoon on Golgotha Road, and the next show was at five-thirty.

That gave him plenty of time. He continued to thumb through tomorrow's news. He came across a small item about supply man József Pereszlényi whose Wartburg (license plate No. CO 75-14) exceeded the speed limit just a few yards from the Blue Lagoon movie

---

* A reference to the film by Milos Forman (1965), the dominant figure of the Czech New Wave.

on Golgotha Road and collided head-on with a truck. The incautious supply man died on the spot.

"Well, I'll be darned," Pereszlényi said to no one in particular. He glanced at his watch. It was almost five-thirty. He shoved the newspaper into his pocket and exceeding the speed limit just a few yards from the Blue Lagoon movie on Golgotha Road collided head-on with a truck. The poor man died with next day's news in his pocket.

professional pride

I'm not made of putty. I know how to get a grip on my-self. Long years of assiduous labor, the recognition of my achievements, my entire future, in fact, hung in the balance, but I kept a straight face.

"I am an animal artist," I said.

"What can you do?" the impresario asked.

"I can imitate the song of birds."

"I am sorry," the impresario said. "That's old hat."

"Old hat? The cooing of the dove? The piping of the reed sparrow? The warbling of the quail? The trill of the nightingale?"

"Passé," the impresario said suppressing a yawn.

"Good bye then," I said with all the politeness I could muster, turned around, and flew out the open window.

there's always hope

"Of course a crypt will cost you, especially along the main route," the clerk cautioned his new customer.

"It doesn't have to be on the main route," the customer explained. "Provided the lining is made of concrete."

"Did you say concrete?" the clerk asked, visibly taken aback. "That is a most unusual request. But it can be attended to."

He pushed the standard price list to the side and made new calculations on a fresh slip of paper. A crypt lined with concrete, even without a tombstone thrown in, and lying on a side path, would still come with a stiff price tag. But the customer said he did not mind. Then he began to bite his nails.

"By the way," he added after some time. "The crypt will have to have a funnel."

"What sort of funnel?" the clerk, who we might add was appropriately dressed in black, asked.

"I'm not sure," the customer confessed. "Something like a chimney. Or a conduit. Or like what they have on boats. Or in wine cellars, if you know what I mean."

The clerk did not know what the customer meant. The engineer who was summoned at this point was not much help either. He had to have everything explained to him twice over, and even then he just hemmed and hawed.

"If I may ask," he ventured, "what should this funnel be made of?"

"That is entirely up to you," the customer said. "You are the expert."

"May I suggest slate?" the engineer said. "Or would you prefer brick? Or plain metal?"

"What do you recommend?" the customer asked.

"Frankly," the engineer said, "I don't understand any of this. Why not stick to slate?"

"Slate will do just fine," the customer said, relieved they had got that out of the way at last. Then occupied with some new problem, he fixed the engineer with his eye. "Ah ... Just one more thing," he added. "The crypt must be wired for electricity."

"Electricity?" the clerk and the engineer piped in unison. "What on earth for?"

"To light up the place," the customer said. "I have a mortal fear of the dark."

an act of kindness

Across from the head nurse's room there are some plastic chairs and next to the chairs a white hospital scale. This is where I generally sit after I get my shot to relieve a stubborn cough. It takes me ten minutes to recover. These ten minutes pass at a snail's pace. Though I usually have a book with me I rarely open it. I prefer to spend the time looking.

The other day two women came down the corridor. They were rather loud. You could tell that the older of the two, who was wearing a light fur coat, must have been discharged from the hospital just a short time before. For one thing, several patients hurried out of one of the rooms to greet her. They were soon joined by a doctor and a couple of nurses. They all talked at once. Clearly, they were happy to see each other. Even the cleaning lady appeared, smiling in the corner.

The reunion took place right in front of me. I don't know why but I always sit in the chair next to the hospital scales. I like to rest my book on my lap and my foot on the scales.

I do not wish to make excuses for what I did. From the fact that the woman got on the scales and from the way the others crowded around her it was clear as day she was going to weigh herself. What is more, her weight was obviously not a matter of indifference either to herself or to her numerous companions. I had plenty of time to take my foot from the scales for the woman, once she was on it, proceeded to remove her coat and hand it to her companion. She then explained in great detail that she was wearing exactly the same dress, shoes and hat she wore when she was weighed upon first entering the hospital. She also said that she was in good health, her appetite was excellent, and she had even managed to put on a couple of pounds.

I will not attempt to explain why in all that time I did not take my foot off the scales. It would require a detailed character analysis and experience has taught me that in such cases explanations just make things worse. As a rule I do not make a habit of putting my foot on scales when other people are weighing themselves, though it has been known to happen.

So, when the woman shouted with great enthusiasm, "See? I've gained ten pounds," I said nothing, though with a few words of apology I could have explained that my left foot had made a contribution, however modest, to her ten pounds.

My silence also had another reason. I did not wish to be a spoil-sport. The woman's expression was one of joy. She received many congratulations including two kisses while she discretely sneaked some money into the pockets of the intern and the nurses. She even had a kind word for the cleaning lady, who was still smiling in her corner. "Thank you too Mrs. Hunyadváry," she said.

And last but not least, somewhere on the periphery of her joy, she also lighted on me.

"What do you think, sir?" she asked.

"I am very impressed," I said.

"Ten pounds, can you imagine?"

"Congratulations," I said.

Then she waved and left with the crowd trailing behind her.

My ten minutes were soon up at which point I also left the ward. Downstairs at the buffet by the main entrance I ran into the woman in the light fur coat. She was holding a paper plate laden with cup cakes. She raised the plate but because her mouth was full with the cup cake, she could only manage a smile.

Ah, so something has begun, I thought. Thanks to me, the woman in the light fur coat has taken the first step down the road to recovery. She was eating again and gaining weight. Of course if instead of gaining weight she should have been loosing it, the whole thing would have backfired. But when you are bent on improving the lot of your fellow men you gotta be prepared to take your chances.

nothing new

One afternoon a nearly seven-hundred pound marble obelisk came crashing down in the public cemetery. It caused an earth-shaking roar, and immediately afterwards the grave (located on Site #14, Plot #27) split open and the deceased, who had been resting there and who went by the name of Mrs. Mihály Hajduska (born Stephanie Nobel, 1827-1848), was resurrected from the dead. The obelisk-shaped tombstone also bore the name of her husband, inscribed in timeworn characters. But he, for reasons that must here remain obscure, was not quite so fortunate.

Because of the gloomy weather, there were few visitors to the cemetery. But all who heard the crash rushed headlong to the spot. Meanwhile, the deceased woman had brushed off the clods of soil from her clothes. She had even borrowed a comb and had rearranged her hair.

A little old lady wearing a black mourning veil inquired after the state of her health.

"It couldn't be better," Mrs. Hajduska said.

"Would you like some water?" a cabbie asked.

"Not just now," Mrs. Hajduska said.

"Considering the lousy quality of the water," the cabbie commented, "I wouldn't recommend it anyway."

45

"Why? What's the matter with the water?" Mrs. Hajduska asked.

"The chlorine," the cabbie said.

"'Too much chlorine," Apostle Barannikov, the Bulgarian florist who hawked his wares at the cemetery gate put in. He'd taken to watering his delicate buds with rainwater, he explained, whereupon someone remarked that as a matter of fact they're chlorinating water all over the place these days.

At this point the conversation ground to a halt.

"What else is new?" Mrs. Hajduska asked.

"Nothing much," those who had assembled around her said.

Another pause followed. Meanwhile the rain began to fall.

"Won't you catch cold?" Dezső Deutsch, the fishing rod maker, inquired of the deceased.

"Oh, that!' she said with a wry smile. "There's nothing like rain for the dead now, is there?"

"That depends on the rain," the little old lady offered.

"I mean this mild summer rain," Mrs. Hajduska explained.

For his part, Apostle Barannikov commented, he was not a party to rain. It drove away his customers.

"Oh, yes, quite, quite," nodded the fishing rod maker. Here another pause followed, longer than before.

"Come now. You must have something to tell me," Mrs. Hajduska said, casting a pleading look at the assembled company.

"What's there to tell?" the little old lady smiled. "There is really nothing very interesting to tell, my dear."

"You mean nothing has happened since the war in 1848?" Mrs. Hajduska marvelled.

"That's not the point," the fishing rod maker said with a dismissive wave of the hand. "You know what they say. There is nothing new under the sun."

"Or to put it another way, such is life," the cabbie added with a philosophical nod. Then, since he had come over in hopes of a fare, he headed back to his cab.

At this point, yet another silence descended on the small gathering. Mrs. Hajduska looked into the grave, which was still gaping wide open at her feet. She lingered a while longer, but seeing that no one had anything more to offer, she decided to take her leave.

"Au revoir," she said as she lowered herself into her familiar resting place. Since he did not wish her to slip on the muddy clay, the fishing rod maker offered her a helping hand.

"Take care now, you hear?" he called cordially after her.

"What happened?" the cabbie asked at the gate. "Don't tell me she climbed back in?"

"She did indeed," the little old lady said incredulously. "And just when we were having such a lovely chat."

e r o t i c i s m

It was a glorious moment in Zsolozsmai's life. Just the other day he had written a review of a play everyone had praised. But he pointed out that the work was teeming with licentious innuendoes, its dialogues were like so many erotic discharges, and in this pan-sexual atmosphere, even the two wings of the curtain seemed to fornicate as they fell.

Zsolozsmai led a life of chastity himself. He had barely ever seen his own naked body. He took his baths in a long white night-shirt in which there was a slit in the crucial spot to correspond with the one on his wife's night-gown. In this manner they were able to bring their three offspring into the world without any appreciable filth to speak of.

The review rocketed Zsolozsmai to the top of his career. He strolled, he floated down Rákóczi Road in the best of spirits. He did not even mind the pornographic displays crowding the street, policemen with outstretched arms, advertising pillars (yuck!), and double buses. Anyone who has ever seen dogs go at it knows what they're up to as they come to a sudden stop.

On this glorious day Zsolozsmai would have taken all this in stride. But just a few steps further down the street, in front of a shop window, he came to a sudden halt.

Behind the glass pane stood a young lady clad in nothing but a tiny bikini, hoisting a red ball above her head. To be sure, the young lady was made of wax. But she made Zsolozsmai, who in the meantime concluded that her nudity was disgusting, shiver all over. He also concluded that for some mysterious reason, her lasciviousness was heightened by the ball she held aloft. What's more, strange as it may seem, the young lady had winked at him.

Instead of walking away, in his embarrassment Zsolozsmai shyly tipped his hat. Then, forgetting he had already done so, he tipped it again, whereupon the young lady laughed invitingly. She shook the price tag from her limbs, crashed through the shop window and flung herself at Zsolozsmai.

The critic broke into a run, but he could not shake off his charming pursuer. Several passers-by took off after them and by the time they reached the Hotel Astoria a fight had broken out. Thinking he was witnessing a political about-face, a newsboy standing on the corner began to shout the names of pre-war newspapers such as *Birth of a Nation and Dawn's Early Light.* This just added fuel to the fire. Unheeding, the bikini-clad young lady continued in pursuit of her prey. She followed him all the way to the university, through the university gate, up the stairs and into a lecture room. There she wrestled Zsolozsmai to the floor and addressed him in these terms: "OOOH, I JUST ADORE YOUR CUTE LITTLE NOSE, PROFESSOR, POOH-POOH-PEE-DOO!" And with that she kissed Zsolozsmai on the tip of his nose and strolled back to the shop window.

e c s t a s y

Lukács Kopp's wife had been laid up with the flu for two days. At noon on the third day the phone rang in Kopp's office. It was a Mrs. Csete or Cseke calling. She said she was the hat-check girl at the dance school next door to the Kopps. She told Kopp that though his wife was feeling much better she was still running a fever. That's why she asked Mrs. Csete (or Cseke) to tell Kopp to take home a loaf of bread and some cold cuts. They needed nothing else.

This commission filled Kopp with a pleasant sense of titillation. His wife Jutka had never asked him to do anything like this before. Jutka was the perfect house-wife. She did all the shopping herself. She cooked, did the dishes, cleaned the house and took care of the laundry. She even looked after their two small children and her ailing mother-in-law. Whenever Kopp, seized by an attack of generosity, offered to help around the house, she always brushed him aside.

Kopp, who had not had to worry his head about shopping for many years, began to make feverish plans. He had just received his two-weeks' pay that day and decided to buy ham instead of the cold cuts, and rolls or milk loaf instead of the bread, or some other type of delicious baked goods. That done, he looked up a friend in Accounting.

"Do you know," he asked, "where I can buy some ham?"

His friend stared.

"In just about any grocery store. They usually have it around the corner."

"Do they?" Kopp asked. Then deep in thought he returned to Insurance.

If buying a little ham is such a problem, he figured, it's no use looking in the small side streets near the office. He'd better take the tram into the City, buy the ham and use the transfer ticket to go home. Since he had no idea when the shops closed he went to his boss and saying his wife was in bed with the flu, asked to be excused an hour early.

He got off the tram at the Franciscans, where he found a grocery store. It was so festive and bright he was gripped by something like a holiday mood, a sense of soaring, like when you enter a well-lit church.

"I'm sure to find ham here," he thought cheerfully.

As he waited in line by the delicatessen counter, he noticed not only the tray of finely-sliced light-pink ham, but right next to it, on another tray, salami sliced just as fine. He decided to buy four slices of ham and four slices of salami, which the salesman measured out for him with the utmost courtesy.

"Anything else, sir?" the salesman asked.

"No, thanks," Kopp said as he shot a sideways glance at the counter. "By the way. What's that?"

"Sausage cream," the salesman said.

God only knows why, but this made Kopp's mouth water. Besides, the sausage cream came in a tube, like toothpaste, and Kopp had never tasted food that came in a tube before.

"I'll take it," he said with some difficulty.

"We also have some lovely Swiss cheese," the salesman said.

This hit Kopp right where it hurt. He was passionately devoted to cheese but he was especially devoted to the Swiss variety. Jutka was aware of this little weakness of his, yet there had not been cheese on their table for years. He never complained. He assumed there was no Swiss cheese in the shops. But now that he laid eyes on the windmill-size colossus, a slice or two already gone, he felt a surge or resentment. "I'll take a hefty chunk of that cheese," he heard himself say.

As the salesman sliced and weighed the cheese, Kopp's anger subsided and was replaced by a touch of remorse. If he bought such a big hunk of cheese for his own pleasure, he thought, Jutka deserved something too.

"What kind of fish have you got?" he asked. Upon the salesman's recommendation he bought two tins of Norwegian sardines and two portions of pike-perch in aspic. He felt distinctly light-headed, though his light-headedness had nothing to do with iron deficiency or sea sickness. It was the light-headedness of a man head over heels in love who had downed two glasses of champagne into the bargain. So when the salesman who by then was in full control of the situation showed Kopp an oval-shaped tin of goose liver paté with truffle, Kopp just nodded. He was beyond words by then.

He was handed his check. He headed for the cashier. He was nearly there when at another counter he spotted some oranges. He took a deep breath and staggered over to the salesgirl behind the counter.

The Kopps lived on a strict budget. Every forint had its appointed place, like numbers in an account book. Their meals were monotonous but Jutka was an admirable house keeper. On the last day of the month their table was almost as fully laden as on payday.

Kopp didn't have to be an insurance expert to look at the sum on the slip he was holding, compare it to the family's daily food allowance and draw the consequences. But Kopp was no longer accountable for his actions. His skin itched. He was flooded by waves of blissful warmth. He no longer thought of Jutka. He thumbed his nose at the world. His eyes glistened, and he silently snapped his ankles together to the rhythm of some csárdás only he could hear.

"I will also take a couple of lemons," he said after the salesgirl had weighed the oranges. "And are those figs?" he asked again. "Don't tell me you have figs?"

Kopp bought the figs and raisins, deep-frozen peaches and raspberries. He was intoxicated. As the assistants and salesgirls weighed, wrapped and reckoned, he hummed a tune. He also bought some spring onions and a bunch of pre-season hothouse radishes. He wanted to buy up the whole world. He danced his way to the cashier where he pinched the cheek of the greyish, white-smocked lady as she was handing him back the change from his hundred-forint bills. He ended up with so many packages, he decided to discard his transfer ticket and take a cab instead.

When he reached home, he put the spoils down

on the kitchen table and went into the bedroom. But by then he had stopped humming.

"You didn't forget the cold cuts, did you dear?" his wife asked.

She went out to the kitchen. When she returned she was as white as a sheet. She stared at her husband.

"Is anything the matter, dear?" she asked, concerned.

"I'm rather dizzy," Kopp admitted.

That's all Jutka needed to hear. She turned up his bed, helped him undress and placed a wet towel on his forehead. She gave him an aspirin. She remembered how in his younger days when he'd had too much to drink her husband always took an aspirin.

Soon Kopp fell into a deep sleep. The next day he appeared at the office with a splitting headache and circles under his eyes. Everybody thought he'd had a night out on the town. And why deny it? Kopp had the impression himself that for the first time in his life, he'd truly had a grand time of it.

self-scrutiny

The first time the man looked in the mirror it was probably just a cloud or possibly some sort of veil or mist that passed before his eyes.

"What's the matter with this mirror?" he asked his cleaning lady.

The cleaning lady wiped the mirror with a rag.

"With this mirror?" she said. "Not a thing."

For some time nothing out of the ordinary happened. Then just as the man had nearly forgotten that little wisp of cloud (or veil or mist) he noticed a fish swim behind his back. He could even tell what kind of fish it was, a four-pound carp, give or take a couple of ounces, a so-called wild carp with scales all over its body.

The man had the mirror resilvered and for years this insured his peace of mind. But gradually his mirror image began to take on a life of its own. For instance, it would wink when the man (or so he thought) did not. Or else it made faces at him, puffing up and deflating its cheeks and the like. The man called up the doctor and asked if anything like this had ever happened before.

"Sure," the doctor said. "There's a precedent for everything." And the good doctor advised him to avoid looking in the mirror.

This was easier said than done, because the man was constantly nagged by the feeling that something was happening in his mirror. But he got the better of his curiosity and resisted looking. Then one day his cleaning lady burst out, "Oh dear, oh dear. Are you feeling quite all right?" This question was prompted by the fact that in the mirror the man's complexion seemed ashen, his cheeks hollow, his eyes the heralds of impending doom. And yet, now that she was looking directly at him, the cleaning lady continued, he looked in the pink of health. In the mirror he didn't look half so promising.

Still, the man would not look in the mirror, though from that moment on it held a greater fascination for him than ever before. When he stood with his back to it, a feeling of deprivation lodged itself in the small of his back. Yet he kept his word to the doctor.

Some time later, and even then only because he was preoccupied, the man stopped in front of the mirror for a quick look. To his horror he saw his mirror image draw a gun from its back pocket, aim, fire and disappear.

When the man stepped up to the mirror and bent down, he saw his mirror image collapse in a heap on the floor with the blood trickling from its heart. And strangest of all, the glass had no trace of a bullet-hole.

the death of the actor

The popular actor Zoltán Zetelaki collapsed and lost consciousness on a street just off Rákóczi Road early this afternoon. Passers-by called an ambulance and rushed him to a nearby clinic. Despite the application of the latest advances known to medical science, including the use of an iron lung, all efforts to revive him were in vain. At six-thirty in the evening, after lengthy agony, the celebrated thespian died and his remains were transferred to the Institute of Anatomy.

Despite this terrible misfortune, tonight's performance of *King Lear* proceeded as usual. Though a few moments late and looking rather the worse for wear during Act I (here and there he had to rely on the prompter), Zetelaki gradually revived and by Act V was so convincing as the dying king, the audience gave him a standing ovation.

After the performance Zetelaki was invited out to dinner, but he declined. "Thank you very much," he said. "But I've had a rather trying day."

in o u r t i m e

"I'll have some coffee," the young woman said.

"And you, sir?" the waitress asked.

"Let me see," the man said looking up at the waitress who was smiling sweetly down at him. "Is it all right if I ask for something out of the ordinary?"

"Yes, sir," the waitress said. "'Though the choice here is rather limited."

"I wasn't thinking of anything quite so out of the ordinary," the man commented.

"Look," the young woman said leaning closer to the man. "If you can't behave yourself, I'm leaving. Must you make a scene?"

Every two or three weeks they had a cup of coffee together, always in the same out of the way place up in Buda, under the chestnut trees.

"Look, Alice," the man said. "You asked for a cup of coffee. Why can't I ask for what I want?"

Having said that, the man turned back to the waitress. "The point is, I know what I want. I just can't think of the name. It's a dark liquid."

"Alcoholic?"

"No. It comes in a small cup. And it's very hot. Which means it can't be anything alcoholic."

"I don't think we have it," the waitress said.

"That's impossible," the man insisted. "Could

"That's impossible," the man insisted. "Could you ask the manager?"

"Yes. But you might as well know," the waitress said darkly, "I have been working in this place for five years." Then she left the table.

"I'm getting fed up with your antics," the young woman said. She hated calling attention to herself so much that even on the bus she'd sit with her head turned to the window. She wouldn't even exchange a pair of shoes if they pinched. "If you don't stop," she warned, "I'm leaving!"

The young man looked into her eyes.

"Why don't you tell me about Yugoslavia?"

At that moment the waitress approached. She had a knowing smile on her face.

"The manager wishes to know if the drink in question wasn't light brown by any chance."

"Definitely not. It was almost black."

"'Where did you last have it?"

"At Gerbeaud's."

"Ah. That's what we thought," the waitress laughed. "Gerbeaud's is a first-class luxury café. We're only a second-class place here. Didn't you see the sign?"

"Wait!" the man said brightening up. "I just remembered. It came with a small spoon. And another thing. There were some small white cubes on the saucer."

"Cubes?" the waitress wondered. Then she laughed good-naturedly. "In five years no one has ever asked for anything quite so intriguing. Cubes. Did you say cubes?"

"Could you please ask the manager?" the man urged the waitress.

The waitress left. But when she reached the kitchen door she looked back, covered her lips with her hand, and giggled.

"Must you make a fool of yourself?" the young woman said.

"Of course not," the man retorted. "So. How was Yugoslavia?"

"Don't pretend you want to hear about Yugoslavia. Now see what you've done!" And she pointed to the waitress who was coming toward them with a stern-looking, bespectacled woman, the manager of the café, in tow. The manager was holding a little-known Hemingway volume in her hand. It was entitled *In Our Time*.

"I hear you have a problem, sir?" she said.

"It's nothing, really."

"We aim to please our customers. What was the nature of those cubes?"

"White. And rather modest in size."

The waitress and manager exchanged a quick look. The waitress, who was afraid to laugh in front of the manager, nevertheless could not suppress a giggle.

The manager kept her composure.

"I am sorry, sir," she said. "But we don't carry cubes of that size."

"Forget it," the man said.

"What's more," the manager added, "I have never come across the liquid in question."

"Never mind," the man said with an exasperated wave of the hand. "You know what? Why don't you just bring me a cup of coffee?"

the redeemer

It was ten in the morning when the writer finally finished his latest play. The night before he still had two tricky scenes left, but drinking one cup of coffee after another and pacing up and down and across the narrow confines of his hotel room, he managed to write through the night. And yet now he felt as refreshed as if he had no body at all, as elated as if life had taken on new meaning, as free as if the world did not even exist.

He made himself another cup of coffee, then walked down to the shore of the nearby lake to look for the old boatman.*

"Will you take me out on the water, Voletnik?" he asked.

"Climb right in," the boatman said.

The sky was overcast but the air was still, the lake smooth and grey and as sleek as a giant pane of Formica. Voletnik rowed with the brisk, economical strokes for which the boatmen of the lake are renowned.

---

* The reference is to Lake Balaton in western Hungary whose shores used to be dotted with union resorts for workers and so-called writers' retreats for those who belonged to the state Writers' Coalition. Here, writers could work free of charge and undisturbed, in idyllic surroundings.

"What do you think," the writer asked after they had rowed for some time. "Can they still see us from the shore?"

"Yes, sir," the boatman said.

They continued rowing. Gradually the trees obscured the red tile roof of the writers' retreat. Only the green of the shoreline and the smoky trail of the train were visible.

"And now?" the writer asked again. "Can they see us now?"

"Yes, sir," the boatman said. "Same as last you asked."

Only the splashing of the oars shattered the profound the silence. No other sounds reached them from the shore. Along the fine line where the lake came to an end the houses, piers and woods merged into one.

"Can they still see us?" the writer urged.

The boatman looked around.

"I don't reckon."

"Good," the writer announced as he kicked off his sandals and stood up in the boat. "In that case, Voletnik, pull in the oars! I want to take a little walk."

r o n d o

She pulls a slip of paper from the
carriage of her typewriter.
She takes two new slips of paper.
She slides a sheet of carbon paper
between them. She types.

She pulls a slip of paper from the
carriage of her typewriter.
She takes two new slips of paper.
She slides a sheet of carbon paper
between them. She types.

She pulls a slip of paper from the
carriage of her typewriter.
She takes two new slips of paper.
She slides a sheet of carbon paper
between them. She types.

She pulls a slip of paper from the
carriage of her typewriter.
She has been working for the same firm
for twenty-five years.
She eats a cold sandwich for lunch.
She lives alone.

Her name is Mrs. Wolf.
Remember the name.
Mrs. Wolf.   Mrs. Wolf.   Mrs. Wolf.

h a r e m

V.P. had eight wives, but because he never got married in the same part of town twice or made a big fuss about it, he avoided calling attention to himself and the fact that in his humble suburban abode he was in fact keeping a harem.

The thing came to light by chance when one of his wives tried to scratch out the eyes of the local policeman, who attempted to enlighten her about the proper way of crossing the street.

In answer to the official summons, seven women appeared before the judge, one Mrs. V.P. born Jolán Maurer, one Mrs. V.P. born Franciska Titeli, as well as Eleonóra Szabó, Mariska Undi, Olga Pipsó and Júlia Ehrlich homemakers, plus the bus driver Géza Soborkuti.

When confronted with the group, the policeman identified Jolán Maurer as his attacker. The judge stood up, looked over the long line of women, then sat down again.

"If you don't mind me asking," he asked turning to V.P., "are all these women your wives?"

V.P. stood before the women with a long whip in his hand. He used it if they whispered or giggled among themselves or in some other manner acted in contempt of court. When he heard the question, he turned to count them.

"Actually, Melinda is missing, Your Honor. But she's on maternity leave. Would you like to see the papers?"

"That won't be necessary," the judge explained. "My interest is purely personal. Tell me. What is polygamy like?"

V.P. pondered for some time before answering. Then he said that polygamy, like anything else, had its ups and downs.

"What do all these women do all day?" the judge asked.

"Oh, nothing out of the ordinary," the polygamist said. "They stand in front of the mirror, gossip, bicker, then make friends again."

"Is it worth keeping so many wives for that?" the judge asked.

"It's got its good side too," V.P. hastened to reassure him.

As he took stock of his wives, he began to list their various advantages. Lórika plays the balalaika, Olga Caroline can do a sword dance. Franci can imitate the murmur of the ocean waves. She just takes a blade of grass between her teeth. Every one of his wives knows something to amuse him. Melinda, the one on maternity leave, smells so strongly of raspberries, it makes your head spin. The judge can't imagine how refreshing that can be on a frosty winter afternoon.

"It sounds tempting," the judge agreed. "However, there must be some drawback to having so many women around."

"All the hungry mouths to feed. The panties by

the dozen. And shoes and dresses. And it's no child's play keeping discipline either!"

At that point, V.P. glanced over his shoulder because his words had been disturbed by the sound of the soft, though not unpleasant, lapping of the waves. He cracked his whip, pulling a blade of grass from between the lips of one of his wives.

"But you," the judge said to Géza Soborkuti who stood modestly to one side, "you are not a woman but a man, unless I am very much mistaken."

The bus driver blushed to the roots of his hair. In his embarrassment he drew a book of tickets out of his pocket and began to tear off the leafs one by one, like the petals of a flower.

"You can tell me," the judge reassured him. "My authority is restricted to traffic violations."

"I am neither a man nor a woman," the bus driver said shyly. "I'm a eunuch."

"And the only one to bring home his pay!" V.P. said appreciatively. "I don't know what we'd do without him."

"I don't understand," the judge said. "If you suffer privation because of them, why must you keep so many wives?"

"Why?" V.P. asked. "But I spend no more on a woman than the next man."

"Yes. But you do it all at the same time," the judge pointed out. "Which is no doubt a great burden."

"What can I do?" V.P. pleaded, looking bemused into the distance over the heads of his wives. "I love dancing, string instruments, the rhythmic lapping of the waves… I like the house when it is teeming with life, when the faces change, and every moment is different from the one that comes before. Monotony would kill me."

"How beautifully spoken!" said the judge pensively. "You are a true poet."

"Possibly," V.P. said. Then cracking his whip, he hoarded his wives down the stairs and onto a passing bus.

stand up and walk
(modern man in crisis)

"We humans never find ourselves
sufficient unto ourselves."
(Karl Jaspers)

"Every moment a hero is buried."
(Sören Kierkegaard)

"Man is not as much as he is but as
much as he is capable of."
*(István Örkény: Letter to Karl Jaspers
and Sören Kierkegaard)*

When the policeman took the vagabond to the police
station, only his pitiful rags held body and soul together.
The left leg of his trousers was missing from the knee
down, and his feet, thin as match sticks, were wrapped
in tissue paper secured with string, just like a piece of
smoked leg of pork.

"Keep away," the captain frowned. "Why don't
you take a bath? You stink."

"I was on my way to the baths when this cop
started hassling me!"

"He was going in there to hide," the policeman
explained. "He was afraid of the mob. They were determined to lynch him."

Then they put the facts pertaining to the case on
record, the long and short of which was that the suspect

got on the No. 77 tram with his fly open. He then put his hand palm up on the seat when Mrs. M. Pál, the principal of a girl's school, was about to sit. The principal jumped up screaming, whereupon the suspect took advantage of her confusion, hiked up her skirt and patted her behind. At this point the outraged passengers forced him off the tram and took off in pursuit.

"That's an outrageous lie!" the suspect protested. "I happen to be Tivadar Tuza, researcher at the Soil Enhancement Station of Gödöllő. I have had my findings published by one Russian and two Italian trade journals!"

"Furthermore," the policeman continued unperturbed, "instead of a ticket, this man handed the driver a piece of aluminum foil that was previously used to pack a chunk of cheese."

"Don't exaggerate," Tuza cut in. "Besides. You should be grateful there's somebody willing to pick the litter up off the footpath."

"Well, don't expect a thank you note," the captain said with a frown. "And calm down. You have only committed a minor misdemeanour. It won't cost you more than two to five-hundred forints. So relax."

"My name carries weight in this business," the researcher warned. "As for me living in sexual deprivation, I insist you put the following names in the records … "

Said list, however, was never completed, because at this point a distinguished looking gentleman entered the room. He was the editor of the *Hall of Fame of Hungarian Sportsmen,* and he had a photographer with

Hungarian Sportsmen, and he had a photographer with him. When he spotted Tuza, he bowed respectfully.

"I saw you getting out of the police van," he said, shaking a finger at him. "I hope you haven't been smuggling watches again!"*

"You know this man?" the captain asked.

"Why, he's Huba Huba the Second, four-time weight-putter Olympic champion!" the editor said to the captain with awe.

The researcher was taken aback.

"There must be some mistake," he said. "I have done a lot of daydreaming about the Olympics, I admit. But I've been suffering from bone decay for years. I can't even play ping-pong."

"Oh, he's always so modest," the distinguished gentleman smiled. Then with the assistance of the photographer, he divested the researcher of his rags, dressed him in sports clothes and handed him a weight. The first put (and without a warm-up, mind you!) was so perfect, it made a gigantic hole in the wall of the interrogation room and snapped the light pole across the street in half.

A coach bearing a foreign licence plate had just pulled up in front of the police station with a delegation from the German Academy of Sciences. But luckily, no one was hurt.

---

* In the fifties and sixties, it was the privilege of politicans and sportsmen to travel abroad. They made a little extra on the side by smuggling into Hungary much desired items such at watches, a fact known to the authorities.

"*Es ist uns eine ausserordetliche Ehre,*" said the President of the Academy to his interpreter, "*den Professor Újhászy, als Wohltäter das Menschheit begrüssen zu können.*"*

"They greet you as the benefactor of mankind," the interpreter explained.

"There must be some mistake," the researcher said. But by then he had been helped into a tuxedo by two Academicians. "Besides, didn't they say Újhászy?"

"They can't manage Hungarian pronunciation," the interpreter smiled. "The visit is in your honor, Professor Újházy, because you have discovered the cure for cancer."

The biologist's voice began to shake.

"Listen to me," he pleaded. "Who among us has not dreamed of freeing mankind from the spectre of cancer? But more's the pity, I am involved in studying the growth of bacteria in natural fertilizers."

At this point the door was thrown open once again and there stood on the threshold the ever-popular TV announcer Marika Takács** armed with cameras, cameramen, and all the necessary paraphernalia needed for making the next instalment of the series, Minor Misdemeanors, Minor Criminals.

As soon as she laid eyes on the biologist, still shaking from head to foot in his excitement, her eyes lit up.

---

* It is a great honor to greed Professor Újhászy, the benefactor of mankind. *(Germ.)*
** Marika Takács, the announcer of Hungary's only TV channel in the seventies, was one of the few real-life protagonists of Örkény's one minute stories.

"Madame!" she shouted with obvious pleasure. "What are you doing here?"

"Who are you talking to?" the captain asked.

"Dear Ágika Knoblauch, otherwise known as Mrs. Kenyeres. Who else? The wonder woman who wins every quiz show on TV. She's even won two trips to Sochi* on the Black Sea. Just imagine! Two!"

"I'm just a simple viewer," Tuza protested. His teeth were chattering. He was in a state. "I wouldn't stand a chance in a million on one of your quiz shows!"

"We'll see," Marika said. "Tell us. Who was the king of the Goths?"

The researcher's forehead was beaded with sweat from the strain.

"Attila the Hun?" he asked uncertainly.

"Congratulations!" Marika Takács said with overwhelming enthusiasm. "We'll begin taping this fascinating interview right now, if you don't mind."

But this endeavor too was nipped in the bud, drowned out by the ear-splitting blaring of trumpets as there appeared with his impressive retinue Dr. Charles Theodore William Lipschütz, chief rabbi of New York's Jewish congregation. At the same time two helicopters flew in the window and began dispersing aid packages of kosher canned meat to the assembled company.

"I have come to the right place, I hope," the chief rabbi of the world's largest congregation said, his voice resonant with the biblical dignity of his office.

---

* Sochi, a resort on the Black Sea in the former Soviet Union, used to be the Riviera of the Eastern Block nations.

"Is this the Sodrony Street police station? The Messiah, we have been told, has come and is presently residing in this very room."

As he said this a briar bush standing in the corner burst into flames. All those present looked on with awe, except Tivadar Tuza, who collapsed with a groan.

The captain made everyone leave the room. Then he ordered some coffee, which promptly brought the researcher of fertilizers around. Once recovered, the researcher decided to come clean. He confessed to his Olympic victories, the vacations in Sochi and his pioneering work in cancer research. He even admitted, however reluctantly, to being the Messiah. On the other hand, he likes to ride the tram for nothing, he said, and if a woman with a tempting behind gets on, he slips a hand under her. This, he explained, is his only pleasure in life.

He was fined two-hundred forints for indecent exposure, but with a commuted sentence. And the captain gave him tram money to get home out of his own pocket.

When he was at the door Tuza turned around, smiled and raised a hand in blessing. "Stand up and walk," he said, then ascended to heaven.

slaughterhouse

First we were taken to the look-out point, which afforded us a breathtaking view of the city. Then we admired the Renaissance courtyard of the presidential palace from where we were conducted to a thermal spring. Here, encouraged by our guide, we tried the spring's bitter but rejuvenating waters. We then boarded the bus again, where the guide praised the loveliness of the Inner City. We also stopped at the National Gallery, where I walked through the rooms displaying their sculpture collection. I was soon in so much pain, however, I was forced to discontinue my museum visit, which meant that I missed out on some beautiful Breughels and Rembrands.

"And now," our guide announced, "we shall visit one of the city's most modern institutions, the slaughterhouse. But don't worry. The animals are dispatched in a very humaine manner, in line with the noblest principles. So the women and children can come along too."

At the slaughterhouse we were led along a huge hall where everything was cheerfully illuminated and where the soft music bounced off the marble walls. There was not a single bellowing or squealing to disturb the mood. Our tour took us from the weighing-in station to the smoked-ham processing station. It was a far cry from what I had expected. I saw no recoiling or snorting animals, nor young, robust butchers eager to wield their heavy bards. The cattle, the pigs and the sheep destined for slaughter were herded from various snow-white corridors into a large room where they grew drowsy, lay down, fell asleep, and passed into the happy hunting grounds as smoothly and peacefully as a boat gliding from the estuary of a river into the standing waters of a mountain lake.

I pulled our guide aside.

"I have a favor to ask you."

"It can't be done, sir."

"But I'm desperate."

"Aren't we all?"

"I won't be ungrateful. If you know what I mean."

"Oh, I've been offered a small fortune, believe me."

"But why is it just the cattle? The pigs? The sheep?" I asked.

"I am sorry, sir," the guide said. "But for some reason, it remains their privilege."

song

The songwriter's name was Jenő Janász. We were thrown together by the Russian offensive of 1944 that smashed his unit and separated me from mine near Niklayevka.* We stayed together for nearly two hundred miles, occasionally catching a ride. But most of the time we marched on foot, through snow and ice, under constant enemy fire, until he was felled by a short burst from an automatic on the outskirts of Byelgorod.**

Up until then I had no idea how songs got to be written. Who would have guessed how easy it was? They came pouring out of Janász, they sprang up, gushing forth like so many springs from the good earth. Anything he saw or heard he turned into song in the blink of an eye complete with lyrics, rhymes and melody. Only the title had to be added.

For instance, once a folk song appeared out of a tin can of fruit preserves we scraped out of the smouldering ruins of a bombed-out warehouse. There was also the bridge blown up right under our noses by the partisans. As we floundered across the ice floes piled

* Niklayevka was a town near Voronezh on the Russian front.
** Byelgorod was a town in Belorussia. After Örkény was taken prisoner of war on the Russian Front in 1943, he was marched to Byelgorod. Some of the details of this one minute story are therefore autobiographical.

under the wrecked remains, Jenő Janász was already singing:

> The old wood bridge o'ver the river it came
> tumbling down, tumbling down
> There's no going back to my beloved town
> beloved town
> Oh my Good Lord why have you driven me
> so far away
> Why have you taken me from the arms
> of my sweet Annie-May?

I asked him how he did it. He said he didn't know. I asked him how many songs he'd written. He didn't know that either. Maybe three, maybe four thousand.

Byelgorod was within view when the snow began to fall. I pulled down my earflaps, but even so I could hear Janász singing in snatches:

> Oh the snow it's floatin' down so sloow-ly
> Russian sleigh bells jinge so merri-ly,
> Flutter, flutter, little flake of sparkling snow ...

Five rapid cracks sounded. Janász was killed, his song left unfinished. At times I remember and try to go on with it. I rack my brain searching for a rhyme to that flake of snow, but to no avail. Each of us can do something no one else can do quite the same way, and that's all there is to it.

m e r r y - g o - r o u n d

The snow squelched under their feet.

"Stephie is a real stunner," Szilágyi said. "She's gorgeous. A looker, if ever there was one."

He walked with effortless ease, as light if he were floating above the ground, a kingfisher gliding over a field of ice. Seeing him from a distance you couldn't help thinking he could even fly if only he'd put his mind to it.

"A looker no doubt," he repeated, wrapped in thought. "But still. She's missing something."

Hajmási stopped in his tracks. These were harsh words from a man who just nineteen months before had confessed to him he was in love with Stephie, just like that, in love, he said. With tight-lipped determination and doggedness he would say no more just this, that he loved her, as if there were no whys or wherefores, no appeals. And now this confession. It came like a bolt from the blue.

Hajmási hurried to catch up.

"What did you say?" he asked. "That she is missing something?"

"Haven't you noticed?"

"I might have," Hajmási said cautiously. "But I don't know her as well as you do. What is she missing?"

Szilágyi looked grave. "I'll tell you. A heart."

Then he stopped. He couldn't help it. He had a habit of swinging his briefcase stuffed with books back and forth, and from time to time it got stuck between his legs.

Preoccupied, they continued trampling through the snow. A little while later, on Rákóczi Road, Hajmási begged Szilágyi to be perfectly objective. They owed it to Stephie, he said.

"We mustn't forget," he went on, "her well proportioned figure, her petite, oval face, her warm, sparkling eyes." As an outsider he wouldn't dream of influencing Szilágyi, he said. But a fact is a fact. There's no way of getting around it.

"What fact do you mean?" Szilágyi asked. "That Stephie is a looker?"

"That's just what I was thinking," Hajmási said. "But I could have never put it quite so well."

Hajmási was not very good at expressing himself. He felt things and the things he felt were legitimate. But he just couldn't find the appropriate words. Not so Szilágyi. He wore his heart on his sleeve. Every one of his observations hit the nail on the head. Like this one: Stephie is a looker.

The recognition quickened Szilágyi's pulse. Proud of himself, he walked with renewed vigor until he got entangled with the bulging briefcase again.

As they approached the corner of Szentkirályi Street his face clouded over and his brow darkened. He said he had a confession to make. But what he was about to reveal must remain a secret.

"Mum's the word," Hajmási said. "Let's hear it."

"I'm afraid," Szilágyi plunged in, lowering his voice, "Stephie's beauty, her up-front, dazzling looks is just an empty shell. Sometimes I look at her and I'm seized with doubt. What's behind it, I wonder? Is there anything behind it at all? Give me your honest opinion, my friend."

"You won't be offended?" Hajmási asked. "You promise?"

Szilágyi promised.

"Well here goes. I say it like it is. Stephie hasn't got a heart. And now I bet you're offended."

For the time being, though, Szilágyi was in no condition to be anything of the kind. He was busy with his briefcase again. Only when they'd reached the corner of St. Roach's Hospital did he admit with a pain in his voice he was powerless to conceal that what Hajmási had just said was all too true. "Of course," he added, attempting to mitigate the harshness of the sentence, "we mustn't forget one thing."

"What?" Hajmási asked.

"That Stephie's a looker. Though I could be biased, of course," Szilágyi added with a heavy heart. "Tell me honestly. Am I biased?"

"You're not biased," Hajmási hastened to assure him. "She has a slender figure, fine curves and a flawless complexion. But something, and don't be offended, for God's sake, yes, something minor, of no consequence, really, is missing from her all the same."

"Yes. A heart," Szilágyi sighed.

"It sounds cruel like this," Hajmási said in order to comfort his distressed friend. "Because let's face it.

to comfort his distressed friend. "Because let's face it. Stephie is a girl of obvious merits."

"I know," Szilágyi said. "She's a looker if ever there was one."

The snow continued to fall. Szilágyi pressed his briefcase under his arm. Hajmási turned up the fur collar of his overcoat. Their conversation promised to be a long one.

m a t h e m a t i c s

The two old friends agreed to go to the Apostles. It was a good restaurant. The distinguished physicist felt like having a glass of vermouth. Szilágyi had a hankering for beer. But man proposes, God disposes, as they say, and so things took a different course. The distinguished physicist had his vermouth since as we all know science and impulse do not mix. Szilágyi, on the other hand, was a born glutton. He threw all caution to the wind. Pretending he did not notice, he consumed five scones. Then he spotted some walnut cake on a tray. After the cake he had a beer. And after the beer it crossed his mind, improbable as the idea may have seemed at the time, that there might be some marinated carp in the kitchen. This, he said after he had finished the carp, satisfied his hunger, more or less. He also ordered chicken soup with vermicelli and a side helping of lentils with a bit of smoked pork. But to give him his due, he merely picked at these delicious morsels. A warm dinner was waiting for him at home. "Let's get the bill," he said, turning to the distinguished physicist. "You know what mother's like. I'm five minutes late for dinner and she gets all worked up. She sits listening for the door bell to ring."

Szilágyi, who could recall every morsel of food he'd consumed in the past five years, told the head-he'd consumed in the past five years, told the head-waiter what he had to eat.

After adding up the bill, the headwaiter placed it discretely on the table.

"Eleven-twenty," he announced.

The distinguished physicist was about to reach for his wallet when his hand stopped in mid-air.

"I hope you don't mind," he said with an angelic smile. "But the sum comes to eleven-ten."

The headwaiter quickly withdrew the slip and with a faint blush added up the column of figures again. Then he looked at the distinguished physicist.

"Beg your pardon, sir, but it is eleven-twenty after all." And he placed the new slip of paper on the table.

The distinguished physicist did not even look at it. Solar systems and Milky Ways revolved in his head. What need had he of paper and pen? So with the ut-most modesty he merely commented that in his humble opinion the headwater's calculations were incorrect. The correct sum came to eleven-ten. And with his an-gelic smile he added, "I am Albert Einstein. So I hope you will excuse my presumption."

The headwaiter gasped. "Oh, dear," he said un-der his breath. He should have known. Such a famous, distinguished face! Bowing profusely, he backed away to a nearby table. He sharpened his pencil, with trem-bling hand took out a larger sheet of paper and with calligraphic precision once again jotted down the num-bers in a row. Then he added them up. He added them up again. And again. His forehead was beaded with perspiration. He stood up and with knees buckling under him withdrew to the back of the restaurant. He called over another waiter as well as Herr Fröhlich, the proprietor of the establishment who, being supplied with graph paper, set about making his own calculations. They put their heads together and consulted in a whisper.

"Deeply honored Professor," Fröhlich said as he reached his table. "It pains me beyond measure to have to tell you this. But according to our feeble calculations the bill comes to eleven-twenty. Please don't think we are being petty. Nothing would please us more than to have you as our guest and foot the bill. However, our headwaiter has been in this business for thirty years. He is the father of four, besides. To him these ten fillérs are a matter of honor."

Professor Einstein nodded indulgently, closed his eyes and in a brief instant made a mental reckoning of the column of figures from the vermouth to the lentils. Then he sighed.

"My friends," he said. "I sit here before you as humbled as Galilei before the Holy See. But what can I do? Science knows no points of honor. Besides, childless as I am, I would be just as ashamed of my mistake as the deeply honored headwaiter is now ashamed of his. In short, this dispute must be settled!"

Fröhlich nodded.

"Nothing would please us more!"

"Possibly," the distinguished physicist said as he continued his rumination, "the problem is we are overburdened with figures and the task at hand is too lowly for our intellects. Is there anyone here who has no college education? Someone who has not even graduated high school and can barely do his sums? Such menial disputes should be settled by the mentally innocent."

As luck would have it, the Apostles had a deaf-mute bartender who was promptly summoned and asked to sit down. Then they put a column of figures in front of him from the vermouth to the lentils and he was told to add them up. The bartender panted, the bartender groaned, the bartender sighed, the bartender sweated. It took him twenty minutes to finish the addition. When he finished, he handed the results to Fröhlich.

Fröhlich glanced at the sheet of paper and passed it to the headwaiter, who passed it to the waiter, who placed it in front of Einstein.

The renowned physicist stood up, counted out the money and left a handsome tip. Then with a modest smile playing on his lips he said, "Gentlemen, Albert Einstein concedes defeat. Good bye."

As Einstein and Szilágyi walked out of the restaurant the staff stood in line and bowed low before the pioneer of modern physics.

Out on the street, Einstein looked careworn.

"What is your opinion of this affair, my friend?" he asked Szilágyi.

"I must be off to dinner," Szilágyi said. "But I can't help feeling that something is definitely amiss."

the right to remain standing

And now if the conductress who under pretense of looking elsewhere has already given me the once-over once
too often with her eyes should happen to say will all
passengers kindly move to the back of the bus then I you
can bet your life wouldn't so much as open my mouth
nor would I move I'd remain standing right where I was
as if my feet were rooted to the spot for which I have a
perfectly legitimate excuse my briefcase is resting against
my ankles with a six-pack of beer ten pairs of franks
mustard bread butter cheese and a bottle of three-star
brandy sixteen pounds in all and I'll be damned if I
move it it's all I can do keeping it from tipping over
every time that madman of a bus driver decides to slam
his foot on the brake and all this because the world is
crammed full of unpredictable insufferable hysterics
like my best friends who would insist on waiting till the
last minute to finagle an invitation to dinner but how
could I explain that here I'd end up making a complete
fool of myself in front of all these people so I will stay
where I am come hell or high water

    so then should the conductress and this is not en-
tirely out of the question happen to address me saying
WILL THAT GENTLEMAN IN THE GREY COAT KINDLY
MAKE ROOM FOR THE BOARDING PASSENGERS I'd
have no alternative but to say firmly politely but with-

out mincing my words madame you'd be well advised to shut up then if hearing this the conductress and this is only to be expected should chance to respond how dare you talk to me like that then I'd chance to respond still politely but with a certain reserve at least madame why don't you turn blue in the face choke on your own spittle but above all SHUT YOUR TRAP because all you do is lecture annoy and insult the passengers and if after this since such things have been known to happen she should retort IF YOU PERSIST IN ADDRESSING ME IN THAT TONE OF VOICE SIR I SHALL BE FORCED TO CALL A COP I'd counter with look here madame you can call the army the navy the entire air force for all I care I will not budge from this spot to which I have as much right as the next man

now then provided she could call a cop at all and the cop could elbow his way onto this crowded bus and accost me I'd say cool as a cucumber but determined all the same I'd say look here friend why don't you go to the devil to which if he and this is also within the realms of possibility should happen to say if you insist on using that tone of voice with me sir I shall be obliged to take you in then I seeing how even my angelic patience has its limits would say look friend you're not taking me anywhere if you know what's good for you or I might just end up mistaking your belly for a trampoline and bounce up and down on it until all the wind's gone out of you and you won't feel like intimidating me any more and if after this which is only to be expected the police captain questioning me should happen to lecture me saying look here my good fellow you look

like a man of learning your clothes and demeanor be-
tray a man of sound sense how could you say such a
thing to an officer of the law who was only doing his
duty when he took a poor working woman into his pro-
tection who was only doing her duty too and with the
utmost courtesy I might add well this I wouldn't even
deign to answer I'd back up a step unzip my fly and pee
on the greasy ink stained institution grey carpet on the
floor of the police station and after having thus relieved
myself and having zipped up my fly at most I'd say
THERE CAPTAIN THAT'S MY ANSWER and if after that
and this is still within the realm of probability the chief
physician of the psychiatric ward should with mock in-
dulgence instruct me to close my eyes stretch out my
arms and head down an imaginary line in his direction I
wouldn't close my eyes I wouldn't stretch out my arms
no instead I'd start down that imaginary line towards
the doctor sure as hell and I'd kick him so hard in the
stomach he'd do a double flip over the top of his desk
AND THAT'S JUST FOR STARTERS because if after this
the muscular male nurse lurking in the background
should throw himself at me to restrain me I and I would
not be taken unawares I assure you would kick him in
the shin so hard he'd fall flat on his back and I'd fling
myself on him pin him down and gouge out his eyes
pressing my two thumbs way in from the sides which
would make his two eye-balls pop out of their sockets
with a soft squelching sound after which just to make
double sure I'd bash his brains in and thus gaining an
escape route I'd take my briefcase hail a cab and be
home in time to greet my dinner guests with my usual
equanimity.

Executioner's Wife: This cheese soufflé is delicious.

Executioner: Light as a feather.

Condemned Man's Wife: You must try the cup cake too.

Executioner's Wife: I've never tasted cup cake quite so mouthwatering before.

Condemned Man: We should get together more often.

Executioner's Wife: It's the only way to learn about each other.

Executioner: Every meeting brings new understanding.

Condemned Man's Wife: We're a small nation. We should stick together.

Condemned Man: Sticking together is what we do best.

Executioner: Shouldn't we be on a first name basis, friends?

Condemned Man: Don't you remember? We already are.

Executioner: I'd like to get to know you better.

Condemned Man: I'll drink to that!

Executioner: To your very good health!

Condemned Man: And to yours, Comrade!

1 9 4 9
(show trial)

Foreign Minister László Rajk, the respected Party man, was sentenced to death today. His execution, carried out at his own request, will take place before a select audience of invited dignitaries.*

* László Rajk was Minister of Foreign Affairs in 1949 when Hungary's Communist Party Secretary Rákosi put him on trial for spying for the western Imperialists. Since such trials had no basis in fact, they quickly became known as Show Trials. One curious aspect of these trials was the way the authorities managed to convince the accused that they must play along for the good of the Communist cause. Hence the reference here to Rajk being executed "at his own request".

h i s t o r i c a l   m i s t a k e

"Hello? Moloko?"

"Excuse me?"

"Moloko?"

"Vy po-russki govorite?" *

"I'm sorry. I don't understand."

"Neither do I, madame."

"I want to speak to my son-in-law."

"In that case, why did you ask for moloko?"

"Why not?"

"Because it's Russian for milk."

"But that's what I call my son-in-law."

"Well, that's not me."

"But I'm sure I dialed the right number."

"In that case, there must be some grave mistake, madame."

---

* "Do you speak Russian?" The short piece is a reference to the absurdity of the Russians "calling" on the Hungarians when they marched into the country in 1944, then forgetting to leave.

the fifties

"Daddy, do you know who has the most
  beautiful name in the whole wide world?"
"No, sweetheart. Who?"
"Vladimir Ilyich Lenin."
"And who told you that?"
"My teacher. Why? Don't you like it, Daddy?"
"Oh, it's lovely, dear."
"Then can we go now, Daddy?"
"Yes, dear. We mustn't be late for Mass."

official government report published in the wake of the triumph of the principles of communism

According to a recent statement by government spokesman Károly K. Károly, István Balogh, Sr., stable boy at the Bábolna State Farmers Co-operative, has just started his regular yearly vacation.*

(MTI Hungarian News Agency)

---

* The Hungarian Communist party's daily newspaper, *Népszabadság*, every year announced, "Kádár János, the First Secretary of the Hungarian Socialist Worker's Party started his regular yearly vacation today".

i n t e r p e l l a t i o n

Dénes Dénes, the MP universally acclaimed for his proposals and interpolations of public interest, was once again preparing a major proposal for the day's session of Parliament. The night before he had busied himself collecting information and in the morning too it's all he could think about as he sipped his coffee in bed.

But possibly because he was preoccupied, the MP for Csenger got the sequence of events confused and instead of taking his bath, he addressed his proposal to end the drought not to Parliament but to his wife and two teenage sons who happened to be in the bathroom. His family unanimously seconded his proposal.

In Parliament, however, when it was his turn to speak Dénes Dénes went up to the speaker's platform, where instead of delivering his interpolation in the interest of bettering the future of his drought-ridden district he took a nice hot bath. He got into the tub, lathered his ears, neck, underarms and loins, and after showering and drying himself, sat back down in the seat tradition had assigned him as Csenger's representative.

After a short debate which included a speech by the Minister of Agriculture, Dénes's proposal was unanimously approved and was immediately enacted into law.

public opinion survey

The Hungarian Public Opinion Research Bureau has just conducted its first survey, the results of which have recently been made public. The question asked was: How do people see the past, present, and future of the nation? In order to insure credible results, the bureau sent out questionnaires to 2,975 citizens of various social standings, ranks, professions and religious persuasions.

The questions were as follows:

1. Your opinion of the present regime is:
   a) favorable
   b) unfavorable
   c) neither favorable nor unfavorable
      but a little improvement wouldn't hurt
   d) I want to move to Vienna.

2. Do you feel alienated?
   a) I feel completely alienated
   b) I feel almost completely alienated
   c) I am, so to speak, pretty thoroughly alienated
   d) from time to time I manage to see the Party Secretary.

3. What are your cultural interests?
    a) I go to the movies, ball games and bars
    b) from time to time I look out the window
    c) I do not even look out the window
    d) I disapproves of Mao Tse Tung's
        Little Red Book.

4. Your philosophical orientation tends toward:
    a) Marxism
    b) anti-Marxism
    c) science fiction
    d) alcoholism.

The results of the survey indicate that the people of Hungary hold the following views in common:

1. During the past twenty years, Hungary has been a paradise on earth.

2. Hungary is still a paradise on earth, except bus No. 9 tends to run behind schedule.

3. Hungary's future will be even brighter provided they add more buses to line No. 9.

proof of character

Since the factory gate was just a couple of yards away, I decided to leave my car at the draw well. The factory I was visiting was surrounded by mountains and the mountains were covered with vineyards, forests and clearings. A high voltage power line cut rudely across the landscape.

In the sixties, outlying factories were like potato patches; they used to be guarded by dogs. Spotting me, the dog snarled. Foaming at the mouth, teeth bared and howling ferociously, it bolted from the gate house and stopped halfway. It cocked its head to the side and picked a choice spot to bite me.

I had been bitten by a sheep dog once, my friend's puli, a pure pedigree. I stopped and tried to assess how a strange sheep dog would bite, a mongrel, a mixed breed like this, whose lesser half only was sheep dog, the rest was pure bloodthirst, disgruntlement, treachery. I looked at the puli and backed away.

I got into my car. When I got up the courage and got out again, the dog advanced. It came weak in the knees, wagging its tail. It looked at me with adulation. It saw I had a car. It raised its head for me to scratch. I obliged him.

"Corrupt cur," thought I.

"Corrupt cur," thought the dog.

professors
before the bench

A court in Budapest has today brought down a verdict in the case of the State contra former college professor Géza Kashka-Kun and sixteen of his accomplices. The professor whose fame has spread beyond the country's borders along with his gang of distinguished physicists, linguists, astronomers, historians, cybernetics experts and Sophia Schleinz, 24, a belly dancer who as La Paloma appeared nightly at the Damascus Bar & Grill were charged with compiling, editing and distributing a two-volume abomination entitled *The Great Hungarian Lexicon.* The court charged that every word of the said lexicon was a fallacious phantasm devoid of any truth content whatsoever and furthermore, that its sole purpose was to mislead an unsuspecting public.

In his appeal the counsel for the defense pointed out the defendants' clean records and impressive scientific achievements. He attempted to demonstrate that at such a high level of accomplishment professional knowhow can all to easily turn into its opposite. The court accepted only one attenuating circumstance, namely, that the lexicon forgers enjoyed no material gains from their publication.

In the view of the public prosecutor, the defendants' educational background and scientific achievements just aggravated the arguments against them, in

100

support of which he proceeded to read several entries from *The Great Hungarian Lexicon.* The scientists, writers and other public notables attending the hearing vented their outrage with loud cries of "Phew!" We present some of the entries below.

BUDAPEST. pop. 1,800,000. Founded by the weaver Antal Valero in 1776 as a silk works and built after blueprints by architect Hildin Valero.* The rest did not turn out so well.

LITERATURE. Medicinal water that surfaces on a swampy goose pasture on the outskirts of the small country town of Pécel. Though effective in the cure of digestive and menopausal disorders, it may be counter-indicated for prostates. Those with hare-lip drink it with a straw, while healthy people are expressly warned against it.

ETHICAL WORLD VIEW. Like soccer, a mass sport engaged in by twenty-two participants. The viewers (sometimes in the tens of thousands) who are not bound by the rules themselves egg the players on. It is no skin off their backs.

HUNGARY. A mania (med. *fixa idea*) with a population of ten million. It is now generally regarded as curable, though this would take away much of its charm.

---

* Antal Valero really did establish a famous silk works in Pest, though in 1783 and not 1776. But he was not the founder of the city, which was first settled in an organized manner by the Romans. Hildin Valero's identity, however, must remain veiled in mystery.

101

HEGEL, Georg Wilheilm Friedrich (1770–1831). German law student and father of several boys (the Young Hegelians). As a consequence of an equilibrium dysfunction, he could not tell the difference between up and down and so from time to time had to be stood on his feet instead of his head.*

THEATRICAL PERFORMANCE. A pleasant way to spend an evening, for which there is no Hungarian equivalent (Ger: *Zerstreuung;* Fr: *distraction,* Eng: *entertainment).* A popular artistic experience elsewhere, at home it is generally regarded as a mild form of euthanasia.

MIKLÓS SZABÓ (1897–1964). Telegram boy and until his retirement a file clerk. He never did anything of note. As the monographs written about him prove, he never had literary ambitions either. He was laid in state in the main hall of Parliament.**

The court sentenced Kashka-Kun to eight years in prison. The other defendants received eighteen months each.

---

* Hegel was the last of the great philosophical system builders of modern times. In a dialectical scheme that swung from thesis to antithesis and back again to a higher synthesis, he found a place for everything, both natural and human. This came in handy for latter-day Marxists who were proponents of "historical inevitability", the idea that Communism was the natural and inevitable consequence of historical development. All they had to do was "stand Hegel on his feet again" – presumably because he saw things upside down.
** This fictitious lexicon entry ridicules the Communists' attempts to make big men of their followers, including workers, who had nothing to their credit except their Party affiliation.

Since she had no prior knowledge that the nude photo taken of her was to illustrate 75 entries of *The Great Hungarian Lexicon,* including the crowning of Queen Victoria, the Laws of Hammurabi and Louis Kossuth going into exile, Miss Schleinz was acquitted.

The verdict is up for appeal.

that certain
stalintown anecdote

Here follows a short item on one of my visits to the in-dustrial showcase Stalintown taken from the newspaper *Magyar Nemzet:* *

"This happened in the early fifties *ad urbe condita,* a couple of years after the industrial city of Stalintown was founded. At the time the huge construction work attracted many questionable, hostile, déclassé elements. Once a well known scientist or artist, he might even have been a writer, it is hard to tell after all these years, visited the town from Pest. He was shown around by one of the functionaries of the Iron Works. The func-tionary was giving him the usual talk full of clichés he had learned by heart. He was dishing it out without thinking, something along these lines. "This will be the colossal industrial citadel of the Hungarian nation, Socialism cast in iron."

Then he remembered the visitor's name. He stopped in mid-sentence. He searched in his store of memories. (For the sake of convenience, let us call the visitor Szabó.)

---

* The story related here in there different versions is based on an actual visit by Örkény to the socialist industrial showcase back in the fifties. I know this for a fact. He told my Aunt Lilly and my Aunt Lilly told me. [*trans.*]

"Szabó. Szabó. You wouldn't happen to be the son of the former textile merchant by any chance?"

"I would," said the visitor.

Whereupon, with a gleeful smile the functionary leaned closer and whispered in his ear, "Well, in that case you might as well know. It's horse shit we'll have here, not steel!"

The writer's corrigendum, sent to the newspaper:

Ernő Mihályfi
Editor-in-Chief
Magyar Nemzet
Budapest

1 June, 1960

My Esteemed Friend,
In Friday's edition of your fine newspaper I came across an anecdote concerning my person. While it is a source of satisfaction to me to be thus remembered within the pages of so illustrious a paper, it would have given me even greater satisfaction had the article been more accurate. Would you therefore be good enough to publish the following corrections at your earliest convenience:

1. My name is not Szabó, but Örkény.

2. My dear departed father was not a textile merchant but the owner of a pharmacy.

3. The functionary in question did not say horse shit, but horse's balls. In point of fact, he said, "It's horse's balls we'll have here, not steel!" [my emphasis]

Thanking you in advance, I remain,

Faithfully yours,
István Örkény

And in the writer's own words:

"I was the subject of a famous anecdote (famous because it reflected the times). And of all places it happened in Stalintown.

'I've come to have a look at the spot where that big foundry is planned, Comrade Engineer.'

'It's right where we are standing now, Comrade Writer.'

'But it's all weeds and trash. When will this ever be turned into a foundry?'

'Thanks to socialist shock-work, Comrade Writer, we'll have the casting by the 20th of August, Constitution Day!'

'That's just two months away, Comrade Engineer and not a spade has yet touched the soil.'

'Don't you worry, Comrade Writer. By August 20th steel will flow here. And did I get it right, Comrade Writer? Is your name Örkény?'

'That's right.'

'The former pharmacist's son?'

'Yes.'

'The owner of the Star Pharmacy before nationali-

106

'The owner of the Star Pharmacy before nationalization?'

'Yes.'

'Is that esteemed gentleman really your father?'

'Yes, indeed.'

'Well, then, that's different!' said the engineer. 'In that case you might as well know. A horse's balls is what we're going to cast here, not steel!'"

portrait of a man

To say my lot couldn't be better would be a gross exaggeration. Not that I have anything to complain about. When I applied at the depot I got hired on the spot and though the pay is peanuts the work is light. All I have to do is watch 5,000 containers of sulphuric acid and several hundred two-hectoliters barrels of industrial alcohol which is kept behind barbed wire. My job is to make sure none of it is stolen, which is fine provided you prevent others from stealing while you walk off with the stuff yourself. It's a darn shame I don't go in for such things any more. But I am a former political prisoner released on amnesty and as you can imagine it just wouldn't do. Anyway, I had to look for a little extra on the side, which was difficult considering my state of mind. My prison experience produced its share of disappointment and I promised myself never to trust anyone again and to starve if I must, but to rely solely on my own initiative.

However, luck was with me from the word go. I answered an ad from the Tímár Street Immunology Clinic. Do I want to give blood, they asked? That's what I'm here for, I said. I have been one of their regulars ever since and I can safely say our relationship has blossomed through the years.

I couldn't furnish you with precise figures. I used

to keep accounts but once in pouring rain my notebook got soaked in my pocket. Anyway, allowing for a narrow margin of error, between 1951 and now I have sold approximately 68 liters of blood to the clinic. As you know, during this time there have been significant fluctuations in price. At first they paid 30 forints per deciliter which under the circumstances was not bad. That's when I got this hat and socks, suspenders and whatnot. Later, when they switched to volunteer donations they cut the price to 25 forints. This meant that even the reliable regular donors deserted the clinic. Then as we all know on the 1st January, 1956, they upped the fee to 50 forints, which is still in effect today.*

I don't wish to make me seem better than I am. But my nature being what it is, I continued giving blood even during the 25 forint times without so much as a peep out of me. That's when a young doctor asked if I'd consider switching to marrow. I inquired if the marrow would exclude the blood but he assured me it would not. And the bone marrow would mean a little extra on the side, something I sorely needed. I do not like badly dressed people and my own undergarments were in a sorry state by then.

It is my understanding that they need bone marrow because the radioactive infections contracted during modern physical research attack the bones and the only hope of cure lies in bone marrow transplants.

* The date is a reference to the ill-fated Revolution which broke out against the Communist regime. In the course of the fights, many people lost their lives, and many more were wounded.

Anyway, I found my reckoning. They give you a shot. All you feel is a little sting in your chest and with the same needle they use to puncture your bone they extract the marrow. They generally draw off 5 cubic centimeters for which they pay you 150 forints. Strictly speaking, this is not a whole lot. But I'm not complaining. I get the money for nothing, really. After all, the lost marrow is regenerated in a matter of three to four months.

I was pleased with my progress. I did not dream my career at the clinic would soar to new heights. But soar it did. The same doctor who let me in on the marrow deal approached me again three years ago and thanks to him I was among the first to be given blood infected with isotopes. I can safely say that here too I stood my ground. In a scientific institution like this, they have no idea how to weed out swindlers, you see, and people with questionable backgrounds who often resort to deception. This is what happened with the isotope-infected blood. As you probably know, when they conduct this test the first day they draw off 20 cubic centimeters of blood, infect it with isotopes, and inject it right back into the bloodstream. Nothing to it and you're 150 forints ahead. An hour later they check you with some sort of counter and to make double sure, draw off another 5 cubic centimeters which gets you an extra 50 forints. So on the first day you're already ahead 200 forints. After that you only have to show up once a week when they take 5 cubic centimeters of blood at 50 forints a shot. It is a crying shame, but the truth is you'll always find those that'll walk off with the 200 forints on the first day and never show up at the clinic again. I can't tell you how many fine experiments have been ruined on account of them.

Learning from bitter experience, the clinic has since instituted certain countermeasures. Now they pay you only 50 forints on the first day. This way, everybody goes through the weekly checks because they get their 200 forints only during the last check, when the tests are negative, what I mean is, when the infection is gone. I am not bringing this up to sing my own praises, believe me. I merely wish to point out that this countermeasure was not introduced on my account.

If I take all this into consideration and add up the year's earnings I still don't end up a Rockefeller or anything. But I have neglected to mention certain minor remunerations which are not considerable in themselves but which help to boost my humble budget. For instance, each time, even when I only give blood, I am given a snack consisting of bread, a piece of processed cheese, a small tin of pork liver paté, two cup cakes and a bottle of pop. I also get reimbursed for my traveling expenses, two tickets for the tram, there and back.

My state of health is satisfactory. By dint of my good fortune, I am optimistic and cheerful but not because I am looking at the future through rose colored glasses. Just as I wouldn't hoodwink others, I wouldn't cheat myself either, one way or another. But if I can go on donating blood and marrow simultaneously for a few more years, and I don't see why not, I shouldn't want for anything essential.

I have achieved all this on my own. I have asked

no one for help and so have been spared the disappointments of the past. I have no harmful habits to speak of. I don't even smoke. There's nothing I like better than a brisk walk. I enjoy the fresh air, the evening crowds on the boulevard and the colorful shop windows. I also appreciate a good rain and a crisp snowfall. I am not particularly put out by a heat wave and never wear a hat. Summer and winter, I wash in cold water. What more could any man want?

letters from hungary

When he died, the famous collector, inventor and historian Dr. Béla Balla left behind an impressive legacy of letters he had written to people throughout the world. Only now, with the systematization of this formidable body of correspondence which includes the answers to his letters has the scope of this great man's interests come to light. Below we publish a small sampling.

From Albert Einstein:

Dear Dr. Balla,
Thank you for your heartfelt concern. I am deeply touched by your efforts to insure that your letter reach me in the middle of the Second World War by way of a Red Cross plane above the skies of a battle-ridden world.

I am very well thank you, though as you so rightly point out I am presently engaged in solving some rather tricky problems of physics. You are also possibly right that a long-haired, playful and high-spirited Hungarian puli dog is just what I need to bring some joy into my busy and stressful life. However, I wonder whether the Swedish Red Cross could really be persuaded to bring said dog from the Hungarian town of Debrecen to these shores. But if you can manage it, I leave the gender of the dog to your discretion.

113

Thanking you in advance for your concern with the state of my mental health, I remain,

Sincerely yours,
Albert Einstein

From Thomas Mann:

Deeply honored Herr Dr. Balla!
You are quite right. I am the author of *The Magic Mountain,* a product of more youthful days. (By the way, I am very pleased you like my book.) However, I am sorry to say, the other point of the wager you have asked me to settle between you and your friend is not as you thought. Thomas, you see, is not my family name and Mann my first name. Contrary to Hungarian custom, here our first name comes first. Accordingly, my name is not Mann Thomas but Thomas Mann. So you will kindly give those three bottles of *schnapps* to your friend.

Thomas Mann
Kilchberg am Zürichsee

From N. A. Krupskaia:

Dear Comrade Balla,
Thank you for your words of encouragement and advice. Unfortunately, because of pressing engagements my husband has not been home in several days and

must, in fact, spend his nights in the Smolnii.* He has therefore not yet been informed of the words of friendship you have addressed to him.

I do not know whether I have construed your letter correctly. My interpreter is a Hungarian prisoner of war who can neither read nor write and has only a smattering of Russian. But if his interpretation is to be believed, you suggest my husband read the works of Karl Marx, especially *Das Kapital,* a copy of which you have included with your letter. It is a pity, but due to the street fighting here the mail comes in fits and starts. This should not worry you, however. Vladimir Ilyich has already studied Marx's works in depth.

I am pleased you follow developments at St. Petersburg "with well-disposed concern", as you say. Also, I wish to put your mind at rest. My husband is not easily offended. So if you find anything else in his work could use improvement, please do not hesitate to write.

Greetings (from Lenin),
N. A. Krupskaia

From Mrs. Adolph Hitler, née Eva Braun:

Herr Balla!
To the eternal glory of the German National Socialist Post Office, I have received your kind letter here in the cellar of the Reichstag despite the fact that the Bolsheviks have surrounded Berlin and the city lies in ruins.

---

* The Smolnii in St. Petersburg was an exclusive girl's boarding school until it was turned into Lenin's revolutionary headquarters during the 1917 Communist takeover.

Your information is correct. The Führer is greatly devoted to graphology and between two bombing raids (it's the only time we can hear each other) I have read him your analysis. He was above all pleased to learn that you discern in his handwriting certain personality traits of which he is especially proud, signs of a sharp mind, decisiveness, gentleness and a love of mankind. He also smiled with satisfaction at your interpretation that the hook in his 'r' prefigures the success of some brave undertaking and the defeat of the Allies. He has suffered a number of vexations of late which coupled with the stale air here in the cellar has turned his complexion pale and his countenance grave. Your wise and persuasive letter has done him a world of good, for which I am most grateful. On the threshold of our final victory,

Heil Hitler!

From Yuri Gagarin:

Briefly, because I do not like to use radio contact for private communication:

1. I do not have a grandfather called Balla, born in the Hungarian town of Komárom.

2. I felt dizzy only immediately after takeoff.

3. I did not bring beer with me, just water.

4. For the purpose you mention I use a bottle which I plug up with a paraffin cork when I'm done.

5. The recipe for chicken paprikásh I will pass on to my wife as soon as I've landed.

Greetings from the cosmos!

From Albert Kajetán Jr.:

Dear Sir:
My family and I wish to thank you for your kind inquiry. But I am sorry to say we are as much in the dark as yourself concerning the reason why anyone would bother to change the name of our street from the great patriotic poet Sándor Petőfi to Albert Kajetán Sr. My dear departed father spent his whole life as a driver (of his own truck), was twice fined for starting a brawl in a tavern and was once ordered to do a prolonged stint of involuntary social work on account of cigarette smuggling. However, we do not think this could be a sufficient reason for naming a street in his honor. We suspect the real reason lies in our father's introverted nature and disinclination to voice his opinion in public. Still, we like to think that in his quiet hours he may have entertained thoughts of such a revolutionary nature as to make his name worthy of immortality.

With best regards,
The Kajetán family

the new tenants

"So that's what you're really like! I'm sorry I ever married you!"

My neighbors, whose name was Román or Révész, had moved in just a week before the incident here related. They had no children, thank God, not even a vacuum cleaner or a floor-polisher. They didn't even have a name-plate on the door. But they did have a television set.

"You're a fine one to talk! Everybody knows you dined with German officers!"

They got home around six in the evening and as soon as they walked through the door they turned on their TV, like they did that night. My tiny kitchen and their living room have a common wall. I put the potato purée on a low frame.

"Everybody knows the fascist concierge put three chalk marks on my door!"

Meanwhile, I stirred the potato purée. Mrs. Bertha, the cleaning lady, comes twice a week and cooks two days of food for me. Before she leaves she explains things as if I were a half-wit. That cold meat there, it's all right, you don't have to do a thing with it. The same goes for the pickles. But you must warm up the potato purée. Repeat after me. I know you. When you write, you're so absent-minded. Don't worry, Mrs. Bertha, I won't. But only on a low flame, mind you. Yes, Mrs. Bertha, on a low flame. And will you stir it properly? I will. And what will you stir it with? A spoon. A wooden spoon? A wooden spoon. And on a low flame? Yes, Mrs. Bertha, on a low flame, Mrs. Bertha, thank you Mrs. Bertha and good bye!

"You've been lying to everybody for twenty years!"

"Be careful! Don't go too far or you'll regret it!"

Watching this sort of anti-fascist love story on television may be fine but here in my tiny kitchen it sounds for all the world like a fight. However, I cannot leave the potato purée. The warmer it gets the more it puffs, pops, bubbles.

"Don't you play the martyr with me! Who was it that reported on his own god-daughter? Well?"

"Go on, say it! I dare you!"

I am almost done. The purée has stopped bubbling. It is now shooting little bursts of white wisps into the air.

"For your information, I have proof!"

"You're bluffing!"

"Look! Look at this! … "

I can hear something creaking, like a drawer being pulled open. Then the sound of running feet, a struggle, a gagging sound. A woman, the lover of the German officer, no doubt, screams.

"Help! He's going to kill me!"

A shot rings out followed by the heavy thud of a body collapsing on the floor. Another shot. And then nothing. My potato purée is ready.

My neighbors never even had a name-plate so

for days whoever comes looking for them ends up ringing my door bell by mistake. The police, the coroner, journalists, photographers, everyone. They didn't even have a TV. The man, whose name was neither Román nor Révész but Rónai, got off with eight years because of some extenuating circumstance. And now the apartment next door is quiet once again.

c o a l

Wednesday. Mr. Vermes's day from apartment 205 to bring the coal up from the cellar. It is also Mr. Király's day. Mr. Király is the concierge. This strict schedule is called for because the six-story building has only two large wicker baskets left. The Vermes and Király families have been given Wednesday afternoon to haul their coal up for the week.

Mr. Vermes and Mr. Király shovel in silence, then start up the steps breathing heavily. Even now, eighteen months after the war, the stairs have still not been repaired. Where there is a step missing, wheezing and panting they take turns regaining their balance. They do not offer to help each other. They do not even acknowledge each other's presence. Their mutual antagonism is beyond words.

Before the war Mr. Vermes owned a music shop with an extensive clientele who bought instruments from him on the instalment plan. The motto "A Piano in Every Home" was his brainchild. He was considered the wealthiest tenant in the building, yet he did not like to pay the concierge to open the gate for him after hours. Whenever he could, he'd rush home before it was locked for the night.

Mr. Király resented this and so smack in the middle of the war informed on the Vermes family. Let it be said to his credit, though, he did this not because the Vermes family had resorted to forged documents in order to prove their impeccable racial origins, but because they were hoarding thirty-three pounds of bacon fat.

Of the thirty-three Mr. Király received three by way of his just reward. Along with the bacon fat, however, other things were also taken from the Vermes home. They lost their rugs and jewelry too. And were it not for Mrs. Vermes's admirable presence of mind, they would have been dragged off as well into the bargain.

But once the war was over the Vermes family informed on their informer and Mr. Király spent eight months in an internment camp. Here he contracted infectious beard poisoning which ravaged his face with scars and boils. He was not much to look at after that and so his wife was put in charge of closing and opening the gate.

Mr. Vermes, the former music store tycoon, now goes from house to house tuning pianos. He and his family live a quiet and unassuming life. There is nothing about them left to inform upon. The only recourse for revenge left to the Királys is to neglect to empty the Vermes's trash cans now and then and to take no notice of their presence.

Mr. Vermes takes no notice of Mr. Király's presence either. Wheezing, he heaves the heavy basket up the cellar steps in silence, then continues on to the second floor. Mr. Király who has three sclerotic vertebrae does not wheeze. He groans. Though he does not have to climb stairs, he must drag his heavy basket of coal to the far end of the yard.

They each take four turns. Mr. Vermes is seized by profound fatigue. He lowers his basket, sits on one of the steps and watches Mr. Király's futile attempt to hoist his own basket on his shoulder.

On this particular Wednesday Mr. Vermes is so tired and apathetic he forgets his vow of silence.

"So then Mr. Király," he says. "So now you see."

"See what?" Mr. Király asks.

"See what's become of us," Mr. Vermes murmurs.

"I sure do," the concierge says. "But it's you and your kind that's to blame."

"What a thing to say!" Mr. Vermes retorts. "We never wanted this."

"Well then who did?" the concierge asks.

"Who?" Mr. Vermes ponders. "Nobody, most probably."

They rest a while longer, then picking up their laden baskets, start up the stairs.

the last cherry pit

After the great catastrophe, there were just four Hungarians left. (In Hungary, that is. Scattered around the rest
of the globe, there were still quite a number.) The four
surviving Hungarians dwelled under a cherry tree, and
a very fine cherry tree it was! It afforded them both fruit
and shade, thought the former only in season. But even
of the four Hungarians one was hard of hearing, while
two stood under police observation. Why this was so
neither of them could recall any more, though from time
to time they'd sigh, "Oh dear, oh dear, we're under police observation!"

Only one of the four had a name. Or rather, only
he could remember it. His name was Sipos. The others
had forgotten theirs a long time ago, along with so much
else. With four people it is not essential that each should
have a name.

Then one day Sipos said, "We really ought to
leave something behind for posterity."

"What on earth for?" asked one of the two men
who stood under police observation.

"So once we're gone, something should remain
for the world to remember us by."

"Who's going to care about us then?" asked the
fourth Hungarian who was neither Sipos nor one of the
two men who stood under police observation. But Sipos

persisted and the other two backed him. Only the fourth insisted that the idea was the most absurd he had ever heard.

The others were mightily offended. "What do you mean?" they asked indignantly. "How can you say such a thing? You're probably not even a true Hungarian!"

"Why?" he countered. "Maybe it's such a god-sent being a Hungarian in this day and age?"

He had a point there. So they stopped bickering and started to rack their brains. What could they leave for posterity? To carve a stone would have required a chisel. If only one of them had a stickpin, they moaned. With it, Sipos reasoned, they could etch a message into the bark of the tree. It would stay in the bark for ever, like a tattoo on a man's skin.

"Why don't we throw a big stone into the air," suggested one of the two Hungarians who stood under police observation.

"Don't be a fool. It'd fall back down," they told him. He did not argue. Poor man, he knew he was short on brains.

"All right," he said to the others after a while. "If you're so clever, why don't you think of something that would last?"

They put their heads together and after a while agreed to hide a cherry pit between two stones so the rain wouldn't wash it away. It wouldn't be much of a memorial, but for want of anything better, it would have to do.

However, they were faced with a problem. While the cherry season lasted, they had eaten all the cherries, crushed the pits into a fine powder, and ate that too, the upshot of which was that they had run out of pits. There wasn't a single pit to be had for love or money.

Just then one of the Hungarians who was neither Sipos nor one of the two men who stood under police observation remembered the cherry. By then, he backed them heart and soul. He couldn't wait to be of help. But the cherry in question grew so high on the highest branch of the cherry tree, they couldn't pick it during the cherry season. It had stayed where it was all this time, shrivelled down to the pit.

The four Hungarians concluded that if they stood on each other's shoulder, they could bring down the solitary cherry anyway. They mapped everything out in fine detail. At the bottom stood one of the two men who was under police observation, the one short on brains but long on brawn. On his shoulder stood the man who was neither Sipos nor was under police observation, and last came Sipos, the flat-chested weakling.

With a great deal of effort he climbed to the top of the column made up of his three companions. Once there, he stretched out to his full height. But by that time, he had forgotten why he had bothered to climb up in the first place. It went straight out of his head. The others shouted to him to bring down the shrivelled cherry, but it was all in vain because he was the one who was hard of hearing.

And so, things came to an impasse. From time to time all four would shout in unison. But even so, the problem persisted, and they stayed just as they were, one Hungarian on top of the other.

one minute biography

When I was born, I was such a beautiful baby the doctor swept me up in his arms and going from room to room, showed me off to the entire hospital. I even smiled, they say, which made the mothers of the other babies sigh with envy.

This happened in 1912, shortly before the outbreak of the First World War, and it was my only uncontested success, I think. From then on my life has been one of continual decline. Not only did I lose much of my extreme good looks, but some of my hair and a few of my teeth as well. What's more, I haven't been able to live up to what the world has expected of me.

I could not carry my plans into effect, nor make full use of my talent. Though I had always wanted to be a writer, my father, who was a pharmacist, insisted I follow in his footsteps. However, even that did not satisfy him. He took it into his head that I should have a better life than his own. So after I became a pharmacist, he sent me back to college to make a chemical engineer of me. This meant another four and a half years of delay before I could indulge my passion for writing.

I had hardly put pen to paper when the war broke out. Hungary declared war on the Soviet Union, and I was taken to the Front. Here, our army was made short shrift of and I found myself a prisoner of the Russians, a

POW. This took another four and a half years out of my life. And when I returned home I was faced with yet further trials which did nothing to ease my way towards a career in writing.

From this it will be seen that what I was able to create under the circumstances, a couple of novels of various lengths, five or six volumes of short stories and two plays, I created more or less in secret, and I did so in the precious few hours I was able to wrench from the inexorable march of history. Perhaps this is why I have always striven for economy and precision, looking for the essence, often in haste. Startled by every ringing of the door bell, I had no reason, ever, to expect anything good either from the mailman or from any other arrival.

This also explains why, though as a new-born infant I may have attained to a perfection of sorts, from that time on I began to lose my luster, to slip and falter, and despite the circumstance that I became better at my trade and gained more and more self-knowledge, I have always been painfully aware of the impossibility of living up to my full potential.

1968